Teaching Stories
The Arabian Nights Adventures
Scorpion Soup
Tales Told to a Melon
The Afghan Notebook
The Caravanserai Stories
Ghoul Brothers
Hourglass
Imaginist
Jinn's Treasure
Jinnlore
Mellified Man
Skeleton Island
Wellspring
When the Sun Forgot to Rise
Outrunning the Reaper
The Cap of Invisibility
On Backgammon Time
The Wondrous Seed
The Paradise Tree
Mouse House
The Hoopoe's Flight
The Old Wind
A Treasury of Tales
Daydreams of an Octopus & Other Stories

Miscellaneous
The Reason to Write
Zigzag Think
Being Myself

Research
Cultural Research
The Middle East Bedside Book
Three Essays

Anthologies
The Anthologies
The Clockmaker's Box
The Tahir Shah Fiction Reader
The Tahir Shah Travel Reader

Edited by
Congress With a Crocodile
A Son of a Son, Volume I
A Son of a Son, Volume II

Screenplays
Casablanca Blues: The Screenplay
Timbuctoo: The Screenplay

TALES TOLD
TO A MELON

TAHIR SHAH

TALES TOLD
TO A MELON

TAHIR SHAH

MMXXII

S
M

Secretum Mundi Publishing Ltd
124 City Road
London
EC1V 2NX
United Kingdom

www.secretum-mundi.com
info@secretum-mundi.com

First published by Secretum Mundi Publishing Ltd, 2022

TALES TOLD TO A MELON

© TAHIR SHAH

Tahir Shah asserts the right to be identified as the Author of the Work
in accordance with the Copyright, Designs and Patents Act 1988.
A CIP catalogue record for this title is available from the British Library.

VERSION 24052022

Visit the author's website:
Tahirshah.com

ISBN 978-1-914960-52-9

This book is for Alexandra,
the kindest, most precious,
and loveliest melon in the world.

PET MELON BUSINESS

WHILE HE WAS living in the Land of Fools, Nasrudin kept a pet melon, which afforded him a great deal of attention.

People would venture to see the pet melon from across the kingdom. They would shower it with gifts. They would pay to have their picture taken with the pet melon, and would buy all manner of souvenirs commemorating their visit, which the wise fool sold them.

One day in the teahouse, the landlord asked when Nasrudin would grow up and start a proper business.

'My dear friend,' answered the wise fool curtly, 'I already have a thriving business. I'm in the "pet melon business".'

Contents

The Melon King   1

A Melon and the Moon   25

Melon Invaders   38

The Melon That Married a Mouse   46

The Pastèque Kingdom   52

Sherlock Melon   67

The Fox, the Dog, and the River's Soul   81

Marsimus Melon   99

Mazubicam and the Melon Treasure   108

The Melon Mountain and the Valiant Ant   122

Melon Think   134

A Melon Curse   144

The Melon That Would Be King   155

The Square Melon   170

The Melon King

Known to his friends as 'The Melon King', Yahya had a mischievous glint in his eye and the most infectious smile.

He'd been born on a rocky scrap of land overlooking the Atlantic shore, back in the days when King Mohammed V was on the throne.

On his head he wore a tattered old hat he'd woven himself from straw, and on his feet were yellow *baboush* slippers, their leather as coarse as his palms.

The first words he ever spoke in my direction were these:

'You've not lived until you have known the life of a melon.'

We were sitting on the porch of his shack close to my home, Dar Khalifa. As the golden summer sun eased low towards the waves, I turned the words over in my mind.

Yahya grinned, his eyes glinting fiery red.

'I'll tell you a secret,' he said.

I leaned in so as to hear all the better.

'Given a chance, a melon will teach you, and it will feed you as well.'

'That's it… the secret?'

Yahya nodded, the side of his face lost in shadow.

I asked what he meant.

He didn't answer, not at first. But then, as the orange orb dipped below the horizon, he said:

'Some things cannot be explained. They must be experienced.'

Again, I probed for an explanation.

The Melon King took out a handkerchief, dabbed it roughly over his face, peered down at the shore, and turned to me.

'I have a gift for you,' he said.

'Thank you, but there's really no need for a gift.'

Stuffing away the cloth, Yahya nudged a thumb and forefinger beneath the band of his tattered old hat, foraged about, and tapped something onto the tabletop.

A black seed. A watermelon seed.

'For you.'

Wondering what exactly I was supposed to do, I gave thanks.

'Should I peel it, or eat it just as it is?' I asked.

Yahya stared across at me in shock.

'*No!*'

'Not peel?'

'*No, no, no…* the seed's not for eating… not until it's grown into a delicious fruit.'

'Then what should I do with it… with my gift?'

'You must plant it,' the Melon King explained.

'Where?'

'In the garden courtyard at your home.'

An hour or so later, I was back at Dar Khalifa, the mansion I'd bought a few years previously, located slap-bang in the middle of a Casablanca shantytown.

My children, Ariane and Timur, found me in the sitting room when they came home from school.

'What's wrong, Baba?' Ariane asked.

I explained how Yahya, the Melon King, had entrusted a seed to me, along with a list of precise instructions.

Timur jerked a thumb at the seed, then at the large courtyard garden outside my library.

'Let's get to it!' he said.

Before I knew it, he and Ariane had fetched a trowel, a watering can, and a long bamboo cane. Having planted tomato seeds at school, they were experts. While I watched, they showed me how to embed the melon seed so that it would grow just right.

Once it was covered in half an inch of soil, the children sprinkled it with water and marked the place with the cane.

'What do we do now?' I asked.

'We wait,' Ariane said firmly.

Timur rolled his eyes.

'We'll die of boredom,' he moaned.

'No we won't!' Ariane shot back.

Running into the kitchen, she grabbed a magnetic evil eye averter from the fridge door, and set it squarely in front of where the seed was interred.

Days passed.

I got on with writing a book about the legacy of stories and storytelling in Morocco. A writer on a deadline shuts out the world, even if there are seeds to be coaxed into melons, and that's what happened.

Ten days after the planting ritual, the kids stomped in from school and hurried into my office where I was fighting procrastination.

'It's growing! It's growing!' they both yelled at once.

'What is?'

'The melon seed!'

We hurried out into the courtyard garden. Following the line of Timur's index finger, I spotted a good-sized shoot. Fresh green, it was seemingly curious, as though new to the world.

Over the weeks, the three of us tended the sapling as it developed into a pleasing little plant, with a single pea-like fruit. Every couple of days we'd sprinkle it with filtered water, shade it from the dazzling summer light, and protect it from the rats, which swarmed in over the walls from the shantytown at night.

As the little sapling grew, I found myself reflecting on Yahya, the Melon King, and on my own unlikely connection with the fruit.

You see, melons, or rather stories connected to melons, have been in my head for as long as I can remember.

It all began when, on my fifth birthday, my father gave me an exquisite box.

Festooned with turquoise mosaics, it was adorned along the edges with ivory beading, was about twelve inches long, and half as wide.

My father said it came from Paghman, the ancestral home of our family in Afghanistan, and had been passed down through generations. I was used to being given dreary wooden blocks and cheap plastic toys, and so the box caught my attention. It was the sort of thing that is sometimes kept away from children because of its delicacy and value.

Laying it on my bed, I carefully removed the lid.

Inside were three orderly sheets of paper, all folded up.

Pulling out the pages, I looked at the lines of type and asked what all the writing meant. My father sat on the edge of my bed and said that the writing was a story, a story as old as the world. He said it was very important and that I'd learn to appreciate it, like one of my friends.

I asked him about the box. I was so small, but I remember his precise words:

'This box is very lovely,' he said. 'You can see the colours, and the work on the sides. But don't be fooled, Tahir Jan, the box is only a container. What's held inside is far, far more precious. One day you'll understand.'

As usual I didn't see what he meant, and didn't know what he was talking about.

To my eyes, the box was the box, and the story on the paper was a story, and no more than that. The gift was put on a high shelf in my bedroom, and from time to time it was brought down to be admired. The pages inside stayed protected by the box, but yellowed with the years. They're still in there, in the very same box, which now sits on my desk in my library.

Sometimes when I feel the need, I open the box, take out the story and read it.

It's called 'The Tale of Melon City'.

Once upon a time, the ruler of a distant land decided to build a magnificent triumphal arch, so that he could ride under it in a grand procession with great pomp and ceremony.

He gave instructions for the arch's design, and work began.

Masons toiled day and night until the great arch was at last ready.

The king had a fabulous cortege assembled of courtiers and royal guards, all dressed in their finest costumes.

The procession moved off, with the king at its head.

But as the great leader rode through the arch, the royal crown was knocked clean off the royal head.

Infuriated, he ordered the master builder to be hanged.

A gallows was constructed in the main square, and the chief builder was led towards it. As he climbed the scaffold's steps, he called out that the fault lay not with him, but rather with the men who'd heaved the blocks into place.

They, in turn, put the blame on the masons who had cut the blocks of stone.

The king had the masons dragged to the palace.

They were ordered to explain themselves on pain of death. The masons insisted the fault lay at the hands of the architect whose blueprint they'd followed.

The architect was summoned.

He insisted he was not to blame, for he'd only followed the plans drawn out by the order of the king. Unsure whom to execute, the king summoned the wisest of his advisers, who was very ancient indeed.

The situation was explained to him in detail.

Just before he was about to give his solution, he expired.

The chief judge was called.

He decreed that the arch itself should be hanged. But because the upper portion had not touched the royal head, it was exempted. So a hangman's noose was brought to the lower portion, in order for it to be punished on behalf of the entire arch.

The executioner tried to attach his noose to the arch, but realized it was far too short. The judge called the rope-maker, but he stated it was the fault of the scaffold, not the rope, for being too short.

Presiding over the confusion, the king saw the impatience of the crowd.

'They want a hanging,' he said anxiously. 'We must find someone who will fit the gallows!'

Every man, woman, and child in the kingdom was measured by a special panel of experts. Even the king's height was measured. By a strange coincidence, the monarch himself was found to be the perfect height for the scaffold.

A victim secured, the crowd calmed down.

Without delay, the king was led up the steps, had the noose slipped round his neck, and was hanged.

According to the kingdom's custom, the next stranger who ventured through the city gates could decide who would be the new monarch. The courtiers ran to the city gate and waited for a stranger to arrive.

They waited and waited, and waited and waited.

Eventually they spotted a man in the distance.

He was riding a donkey backwards.

As soon as he passed through the great city gate, the prime minister scurried up and asked him to choose the next king.

The man, who was a travelling idiot, said, 'A melon.' He said this because he always said 'a melon' to anything that was asked of him. For he liked to eat melons very much.

And so it came about that a melon was crowned king.

All these events happened long, long ago.

A melon is still king of the country and, when foreigners visit and ask why a melon is the ruler, they say it's because of tradition, that the king prefers to be a melon and that they, as humble subjects, have no power to change his mind.

One afternoon, once we'd tended to the precious young melon, I told Ariane and Timur the story of Melon City, the tale I'd kept protected in a box since I was their age.

Ariane said the melon wasn't actually a melon at all, but that it was a time machine in disguise. Each night, she whispered, it turned back from a melon into itself, and would crisscross time and space, seeking answers from the universe.

I asked how such information had reached her ears.

'The melon told me,' she said.

As the melon grew, so did interest in it.

All of a sudden it seemed that everyone had an opinion on how to care for the fruit, which had now swelled to the size of a tennis ball.

Zohra, our housekeeper, blustered out of the kitchen and insisted we tie scraps of red cloth to the leaves. She warned that if we failed to follow her advice, the melon would poison anyone who tasted it.

Next on the scene was Abdullah, the chief guardian.

He claimed that a female jinn living under the courtyard garden had already laid claim to the melon. If the fruit wasn't presented to her on a bed of vine leaves, he said, the entire house was in danger of being turned into dust.

The next morning, there was a knock at Dar Khalifa's main door. The guardians were nowhere to be seen, so I ventured out to check who was there.

It was the Melon King.

'Everyone's talking about your melon,' he said.

'*Everyone?*'

'Yes.'

'Everyone *who?*'

'Everyone worth listening to.'

I invited Yahya inside.

We made our way through the house and into the courtyard garden where water, issuing from a magnificent mosaic fountain on the far wall, cooled the air.

As soon as the Melon King set eyes on the fruit, he grinned a Cheshire cat grin.

'You've done well,' he said.

'My children have been helping me,' I muttered modestly.

'So you've all done well.'

'D'you think we are watering it too much?' I asked.

Yahya touched a hand to the soil.

'Perfect.'

'What about the sunlight? Are we giving it enough?'

'Plenty.'

I sighed with relief.

As we stood there, both gazing at the little melon, Yahya winked.

'There's a secret to growing melons,' he said.

'The secret that's made you the Melon King?'

'Yes.'

'Is there any way that part of the secret could be passed on to three novice melon growers like us?'

Yahya grinned all the wider.

'You must talk to your melons,' he said.

'That's it? That's the secret?'

The Melon King nodded.

'What do you tell them?'

'Anything you like. You can read from the newspaper, or talk about your life and adventures, but there's something they like most of all.'

'*What?*'

'Stories.'

'What kind of stories?'

'Stories about melons.'

'I've already told the story of Melon City,' I said brightly.

'To the melon?'

'Well, kind of. I told it to my kids… and I'm pretty sure the melon heard.'

'That's not the same thing. You must speak directly to the melon.'

I scratched my head.

'But I don't know any other stories about melons.'

'Then make them up,' Yahya said.

So I did.

Over the next weeks I told the melon growing in the courtyard garden tales about melon kings and queens, melon warriors, melon explorers, and even one about a princess who was wedded to a dashing prince, transformed into a melon by a wicked witch.

I couldn't say for sure whether the melon we'd reared from a seed was benefiting from all the attention. What was more certain was that day by day it continued to grow, until it was the size of a football.

Each afternoon, when the kids came in from school, we poured a full bucket of water over the ground on which the melon was growing.

Then, in what had become an evening ritual, I recounted a new tale.

When my father died, I inherited his library, containing hundreds of books of stories gathered from all corners of the world. After Yahya's visit I'd scoured them for tales of melons, but had only come up with two or three. So, in my desperation to keep the fruit happy, I wrote this manuscript.

The stories I wrote on melons were inspired by oral folklore passed to me by Zohra, the guardians, the blacksmith, and a host of others who were on the payroll. As anyone who's ever renovated a sprawling mansion set squarely in the middle of a Casablanca shantytown knows, hiring people in Morocco is as easy as laying them off is challenging.

Little by little, the tales of melons sewed themselves together into a patchwork quilt of wonder – a quilt as much about ancient threads of life as it was about pleasing a watermelon that was swelling by the day.

Many weeks after we had planted Yahya's seed, the melon was enormous.

Ariane carried the scales down from the bathroom. With some difficulty, we managed to slip them beneath it.

Triumphantly, Timur called out the weight:

'Eleven and a half kilogrammes!'

'D'you think it's ready?' I probed.

'Ready for what, Baba?' Ariane asked.

'Ready to eat.'

As soon as the words left my mouth, Ariane and Timur burst into tears.

'You can't eat Alexandra!' they bawled.

'*Alexandra*? Who's Alexandra?'

'The melon.'

'But melons don't have names,' I said.

'*Our* melon does,' Timur replied pointedly. 'We love her.'

Ariane glowered at me.

'She's our pet melon, and no one's ever going to kill her and eat her.'

Lowering myself down on the step beneath the fountain, I coaxed the children to cluster round. We sat in silence for a long time, listening to the water flowing, and staring at Alexandra. Striped green and white, her taut skin seemed to gleam in the yellow afternoon sunshine.

'Last night I had a dream,' I said.

'A nice one?' Ariane queried.

'A very nice one.'

'What was it?'

'I dreamt that Alexandra was the kindest, happiest melon in all the world.'

'That's because she is,' Timur blurted.

'I know she is. And that's how I dreamt her being. I want to promise you both something.'

'What, Baba?'

'That if we let Alexandra do what she's supposed to do – to refresh our friends in the shantytown – I'll make sure no one ever forgets her.'

'How will you do that?'

Leading Ariane and Timur through the carved cedar doors into my library, I held up a wad of papers on my desk.

'Because of *this*.'

'What is it?'

'It's a little book I've written in honour of the cleverest, kindest, most beautiful melon that ever lived.'

The next evening, we got dressed up in our best clothes and sent a message for Yahya to join us, along with Zohra, the blacksmith, the guardians, and all the others who'd squirmed their way onto Dar Khalifa's payroll.

Ariane and Timur had filled a little basket with pink and white rose petals they'd collected from the garden. Standing beside their pet melon, they showered it in petals while singing a song they'd made up on the way home from school.

As we all clustered around, the Melon King said a blessing, and gave thanks to the courtyard garden for nurturing such a magnificent fruit.

Then, pulling a penknife from his belt, Yahya clipped the melon free.

A moment later, it had been cleaved into slices, which were passed from hand to hand. There was so much melon that a stream of people flooded in from the shantytown to quench their thirst on Alexandra.

Ariane and Timur had been reluctant to taste their pet. But, seeing mile-wide grins on all the faces, they gave in and feasted as well.

'Delicious,' Timur said.

'Refreshing,' Ariane added.

One by one, the visitors gave thanks and filed away into the night.

Yahya was the last to leave.

The children and I walked him to the door, the air fragrant with datura flowers. Pausing, he gave sincere thanks.

'Some people think melon seeds are worthless, but they're not,' he said. 'They're a reflection of Morocco. Give them the right conditions, love them as you've done… tell them stories and sing to them… and they'll return all you've given them a thousand times over.'

Stooping down to their height, he presented Ariane and Timur with a little bag packed with damp melon seeds – seeds harvested from their beloved Alexandra.

'Plant some of these tomorrow,' he said in no more than a whisper. 'Before you know it, you'll have an entire field of melons.'

'Can we give them all names?' Ariane asked.

'Of course you can.'

'Can we keep them as pets?' Timur whispered.

'Yes.'

'But what happens when our melons are eaten?'

Yahya, the Melon King, broke into laughter.

'Save the seeds, plant them, and the magic will begin all over again,' he said.

A Melon and the Moon

ONCE UPON A time in a field not far away, a fabulous crop of honeydew melons was growing, all ripe and golden yellow, and ready to be plucked.

Such was the organization of the farmer, and the fact thieves prowled the fields at night, that each melon was given a number. So, if a single one of the precious fruits was to go missing, its absence would be spotted right away.

By day, the farmer would pace up and down, delighting in the glorious crop. And, as he did so, he would thank his forebears for passing down the tricks of the trade which had allowed him to be a champion melon farmer.

By night, the farmer would sit by the fire in his cottage, smoking his pipe, hoping that one of the fine melons would win a prize at the county fair.

But there was something else on his mind as well.

Whereas the other farmers in the valley were preoccupied with their melons getting enough sunshine so that they ripened well, the meticulous farmer with the field not so very far away was not concerned with sunlight…

…so much as moonlight.

A hundred generations before, the very same field was tended by an ancestor, equally meticulous by nature. An ancestor who had noticed something quite extraordinary:

The more moonlight a melon receives in the hours of darkness, the more exquisite the taste. So precious was the secret to the farmer and his ancestral line, that it was never written down, nor was it imparted to anyone but members of the family.

Before turning in for the night, the farmer did what he did each evening.

He climbed up onto the roof of his cottage and gazed up at the sky.

To his delight, the full moon was shining down from the nocturnal firmament, its platinum light bathing the crop, touching it with alchemy.

Dead centre in the middle of the field was an especially fine melon, numbered in the farmer's hand...

Honeydew No. 54931

Like all the other melons in the field, it had grown from a seed, feasting on cool, clear water from the mountains, and on the finest nutrients in the soil. Like all the melons that had ever been raised in the field, it had dreamt of the life it would have when it was fully grown.

For, like all the other melons in the history of the field, Honeydew No. 54931 believed that, once grown, it would embark on adventures beyond the horizon. The last thing it ever imagined was that it would be put in a wagon, taken to market, and sold to be eaten.

While the farmer slept, the pristine young melon, positioned dead centre in the field, thanked providence for providing him with such a fine existence.

First, he gave thanks for the water that ran down from the mountains.

Then he gave thanks for the most excellent nutrients in the soil.

After that, he gave thanks for the one thing that affected the taste of the melons…

The moonlight.

Cocking back his head, the young melon called up to the dazzling disc of ivory:

'Over months, I have gazed up at you, in awe and in wonder! Thank you, O Great Moon! Thank you for bathing me in your light, and thank you for being as magnificent as you are!'

Now, for a hundred generations, melons had grown in the field – a great many lifetimes, at least in melon years.

The moon had shone down from the heavens for far longer still. And, in all that time, she had been praised, trusted with secrets, and even cursed.

But never in all that time had a melon called up to her and expressed sincere thanks.

Once Honeydew No. 54931 had given thanks for the water, the soil, and for the moon, he closed his eyes and began to drift off into sleep.

As he dreamt of all the fun he would have on his grand adventures, he heard something.

It wasn't a sound from dreamscape.

Rather, it was a voice in the sky.

'You're a very kind little melon,' said the voice.

Honeydew No. 54931 opened one eye, then the other.

'Who's there?' he said.

'It's me.'

'Me *who*?'

'Me up here in the heavens.'

The melon cocked his head up as hard as he could do.

'Oh, my goodness,' he said.

Shining down most brilliantly, the moon smiled.

'In all my nights, I've never been thanked by a melon,' she said. 'Come to think of it, no piece of fruit has ever thanked me at all.'

'Good manners are important,' Honeydew No. 54931 said. 'Where would we be without them?'

The moon sighed.

'Well said,' she intoned.

Silence prevailed for a while and, her radiance brighter than on any night she could remember, the moon spoke to the melon once again.

'What do you dream of at night?' she asked.

At once, Honeydew No. 54931 shot back an answer:

'As soon as the farmer has clipped me from the vine, I'm going to set off on my travels,' he said brightly. 'First, I'll venture beyond the horizon, and then I'll get passage on a ship and will cross a hundred oceans!'

The moon sighed again.

Unlike the young melon, she'd seen the future of every piece of fruit that ever left the field.

'I hate to tell you this,' she said. 'But any day now, the farmer will indeed clip you from the vine. Then he and his team will load you onto a cart, take you to the market, and sell you.'

'Sell me?'

'Yes.'

'Sell me to whom?'

'Sell you to a family, who will take you to their home.'

'And what will they do with me there?' the melon asked.

'They'll gobble you up,' said the moon.

31

Honeydew No. 54931 let out a cry, as shrill as it was despondent.

'But I don't want to be eaten,' he said. 'I don't want to be eaten one little bit. You see, I have grand plans to reach the horizon, and then to cross a hundred oceans.'

'Unlikely,' the moon said.

The melon whimpered a second time.

'Well, what I am to do, then?' he asked.

The moon cleared her throat.

'I've been up here in the heavens for as long as I can remember,' she explained. 'In all that time, I have seen many millions of melons, all like you, each one grown from a seed, then snipped from the vine when they're nice and ripe. Each one of them was loaded aboard a cart, taken to market, sold, carved up, and devoured.'

Honeydew No. 54931 wept a tear.

'Surely, in all that time,' he said, 'at least one of the melons got away.'

The moon clicked her tongue.

'Not a single one.'

'There must be a way I can escape,' he said. 'As I've told you, I have grand plans... grand plans which are awaiting me.'

The moon thought long and hard.

'I was touched by your good manners,' she said at length. 'So I'm going to help you.'

'Help me to do what?'

'Help you to reach the horizon, and travel the oceans. All you have to do is to follow the instructions I shall give you. But remember, when morning comes, I will not be able to help you, because I won't be here until nightfall.'

The moon spent the remainder of the night telling Honeydew No. 54931 exactly what he needed to do.

With dawn, the moon melted away and the sun rose.

When it was high, the farmhands arrived at the field with a cart.

In no time at all, they began clipping the melons from their vines and tossing them up onto the cart. As soon as the first cart was filled, a second was brought, and after it, a third.

Little by little, the perfect rows of numbered melons were cleared.

By late afternoon, the wheels of the cart were nearing the middle of the field.

As instructed by the moon, Honeydew No. 54931 waited for the farmer's knife to clip him from the vine. As soon as he was free, he rolled under a huge melon leaf.

A moment later, the farmhands and the cart were gone.

So were all the melons.

For the first time in his short life, Honeydew No. 54931 was free.

Buoyed by the thought of all the adventures he was about to have, the melon did as he had been told to do. The next step was to wait for the farmer's dog to wake up from her afternoon nap in the shade, and to make her way through the field.

Just as the moon had said, the dog woke up, shook herself awake, and trotted off through the field.

As she neared the spot where Honeydew No. 54931 was hiding under the leaf, the melon called out.

'Dog, dog! You don't know me but I'm a well-mannered young melon and greet you in peace!'

The dog paused. Lowering her head, she feared a trap.

'I know where the most delicious and succulent bone has been buried,' the melon said. 'And I'm going to tell you exactly where it is.'

'Since when did melons like you help hounds like me?!' growled the dog.

'I realize that most melons don't help dogs,' Honeydew No. 54931 replied. 'But most melons don't have fine ambitions.'

'And what fine ambition could you have?'

'I am to embark on a grand adventure,' the melon explained. 'I'm going to cross the horizon and after that I'll cross a hundred oceans. Before I do either, I am going to tell you where to find the delicious and succulent bone.'

True to his word, the melon told the dog where to dig.

In less time than it takes to tell, the bone was unearthed and the dog was feasting on delicious marrow, the kind that tired old dogs dream of while sleeping in the shade.

Once the dog had feasted, she plodded back to the melon, which was still hiding under the leaf.

'What do you want in return for that bone, which I have so enjoyed?' she said.

The melon explained:

'Beside the spot where the bone was buried is a treasure,' he said.

'I would be most grateful if you could dig it up and bring me half.'

'What about the other half?' asked the dog.

'Present it to your master, and he'll reward you with as many bones as you can eat.'

The dog did as she was asked.

By nightfall, Honeydew No. 54931 had used his share of the treasure to purchase a horse and cart of his own.

Next day, he traversed the horizon.

Not long after, he reached the shore. Buying the most magnificent ship in the port, he set off on his travels.

For a good many melon years, Honeydew No. 54931 crisscrossed a hundred oceans.

Each night, he would sit on deck. Cuddled in a blanket, he would gaze up at the heavens, basking in the light of his dear nocturnal friend, the moon.

Melon Invaders

ONCE UPON A time, the queen of a distant land had a dream – a dream that was to change the course of history.

She dreamt that the neighbouring kingdom was about to invade, leaving death and destitution in their wake.

Terrified out of her wits, she rushed through the palace's private apartments.

'They're coming! They're coming!' she wailed.

'Who are coming, my dear?' the king asked tenderly as he sipped his morning tea.

'Invaders are coming! They're planning to attack from the south and from the north!'

The king regarded his wife with concern. His brow furrowed, he asked:

'My dearest, please explain to me how you

have come to be in the possession of such information?'

Eyes ringed with fear, the queen responded:

'All I can tell you is that I saw the invaders with my own eyes!'

Resting the porcelain teacup on its saucer, the king clicked his fingers.

An instant later, the ear of his vizier was pressed to his lips.

The king whispered an order, and the vizier hurried away.

'If there are troops on the border to the north and the border to the south,' he said, 'we shall deal with them.'

Again, the queen wailed, the thought of an invasion too much for her to bear.

Spies were dispatched to the north, the south, the east, and the west. Every inch of frontier was checked and checked again.

Then, one by one, the spies reported back to the

ear of the vizier, who reported back to the ear of the king.

That evening, as he prepared for bed, the monarch smoothed a hand over his wife's cheek.

'There are no invaders, my beloved,' he said.

The queen began wailing again.

'But there are! There are thousands of them, each one armed with swords and spears!'

'Well, they must have turned on their heels and fled, and thank God for it!'

The queen was about to climb into bed when she remembered something.

A small detail.

A small detail that had the possibility of sounding preposterous.

'The invaders were not human,' she whispered.

Again, the king's brow furrowed, deeper than it had furrowed that morning.

'My beloved,' he uttered. 'If they were not human, what were they?'

'They were like some phantasmagorical apparition.'

Sitting on the corner of the bed, his brow beading with perspiration, the king begged his wife to provide a description.

The queen closed her eyes.

And, concentrating with great care, she said:

'They're green.'

'*Green*?'

'Yes, my love. As green as the moss on the walls of a mountain cave.'

'Is there anything else you can tell me?'

'They are not soft and mortal, as we are,' the queen said, squirming back against the pillows. 'Rather, they are hard like drums. And when they're sliced open in the terror of battle, they're as red as red can be.'

The lids quivering over her eyes, the queen let out the most tortured wail of her life. A single ribbon of piercing sound, it was heard through the palace and across the kingdom.

'Tell me, my beloved, what information gives you cause to be filled with such anguish?'

'The invaders,' the queen spoke. 'The *green* invaders…'

'What of them?'

'It's that, when they are lanced open in battle… the battle they will face with our own brave troops…'

'Yes…?'

'They'll be red as red can be… and…'

'*And…?*'

'And, despite fighting the temptation, our soldiers will be unable to resist the most deranged and wretched behaviour!'

'I don't understand,' said the king. 'What behaviour will our brave warriors be unable to resist?'

Her face inches away from that of her husband, the queen gasped.

'Our soldiers will resort to devouring the bodies of the dead!'

Frozen like a statue, the king dared not breathe, let alone speak.

In a breath so frail as to give no volume to a single word, he said:

'Horror!'

Trembling, tears rolling down her face, the queen nodded.

'Our brave soldiers will feast on the flesh of the fallen,' she said.

Next morning, the king doubled the guard on frontiers and went to the barracks to address the troops. Having explained that intelligence had suggested an invasion of green insurgents was imminent, he thrust both fists in the air like pistons.

'If you engage in war with the wicked green threat, you are forbidden to devour the bodies of the vanquished!' he exclaimed.

Back in the palace, the queen had just woken from another dream.

Or, rather, from another nightmare.

Wailing again as she ran through the royal apartment, she threw herself into the arms of the king, who had just returned from addressing the troops.

'They are already here!' she wailed.

'Who are, my love?'

'The green invaders!'

'Where are they?' the king enquired, striding over to the balcony so as to survey the town.

'They're in the markets and the homes, in the teahouses and in the fields!'

The king's brow furrowed deeper than it had ever furrowed before.

'They are in disguise,' the queen whispered, the words spoken in a cold, clear voice.

'In what disguise?'

The queen stepped forwards to her husband and looked him in the eye.

'The invaders are disguised as melons!' she bawled.

In the days that followed, by order of the monarch, every melon in the kingdom was rounded up, transported to the frontier, and left in no man's land.

On seeing so many thousands of melons presented for no reason, the king of the neighbouring kingdom rethought the plans of invasion – plans that were in actual fact quite real.

Instead of invading, he had all the farmers in the land gather up the entire crop of pomegranates and transport them to the no man's land.

News of the gift was relayed to the palace, where the king was still consoling his wife.

Tenderly, the monarch's lips pressed against the queen's brow.

'It's all thanks to you, my dear, that our kingdom has been saved!'

The Melon That Married a Mouse

ONCE UPON A time, a melon fell in love with a mouse.

Wooed as she had never been wooed before, the mouse fell under the spell of the melon's charms.

Day and night the melon would declare his affection for the lovely little rodent, in poetry as sweet as a summer's day.

And, night and day, the mouse would yearn for the time when they could be together as husband and wife, melon and mouse.

When they had been courting for a good long while, the melon got down on one knee and proposed.

'My darling mouse, would you do me the honour of being my wife, and live with me for the rest of my days?'

'Yes! Yes! Yes!' sobbed the mouse.

Overcome, she wept with joy, and was hugged by her beloved harder than she had ever been hugged by anyone at all.

In the days that followed, the melon wrote pages and pages of poetry, echoing his sense of happiness.

And they got down to planning the wedding.

The first obstacle was finding a priest who would marry them.

After all, the Mouse Church and the Melon Church were quite different denominations. The melon and the mouse traipsed from mouse church to mouse church, and from melon church to melon church.

In many, they were shunned for even posing the question they posed.

In others, they were scorned.

Once in a while, they were scolded for bringing sacred values into disrepute.

'But we're in love!' the mouse wailed each time.

'And we want to be married!' her melon fiancé groaned.

Many weeks passed, in which the melon and the mouse were sent from pillar to post. Despite all the uncertainty, they were more committed than ever, their love never faltering for a moment.

'You are like a dainty little melon seed, all shiny and bright,' the melon declared.

'And you, my dear, are like a magical little nest beneath the floorboards, all cosy and warm,' cooed the mouse.

As the weeks passed, the melon and the mouse would take time to stroll together along the riverbank. They would swap secrets and dreams, and would talk about the life they would live once the marriage ceremony was behind them.

At long last they found a minister who agreed to marry them.

A portly lemur with a lisp, his one caveat was that there be a magnificent feast to accompany the festivities. For, as everyone knows, lemur preachers like nothing more than gorging themselves at someone else's expense.

The melon and the mouse were more thrilled than they had ever been, delirious at the prospect of finally being husband and wife.

With so much to take care of, the mouse bride-to-be asked her mother to handle the banquet, which is so important at mouse weddings. And the melon groom-to-be asked his father to take care of the music and other traditions, which are so important to melon weddings.

The invitations were sent out to a hundred melons and a hundred mice.

Huge anticipation followed, the respected guests dressing in their very best finery.

On one side of the church were the melons, and on the other, the mice.

Once the congregation was all seated, the mouse bride was walked down the aisle by her father, and met at the altar by the melon groom and his best man.

The portly lemur stepped forwards.

Vows were swapped.

Hymns were sung.

Bells rang out.

Confetti was thrown.

And then the banquet began.

But it was then that the problems started.

The reason was tradition.

Or, rather, a difference in tradition.

At their weddings, mice tend to dine on slices of delicious melon.

And, at their weddings, melons snap mouse traps to ward away bad spirits.

No sooner had the mouse and the melon been wed, than the banquet brought a swift end to a hundred well-dressed mouse guests, and as many melon guests, equally bedecked in wedding finery.

As for the bride and groom, such was their love for one another that they missed the banquet altogether.

Seizing the moment, they'd sailed away on a boat made from a basin – a boat on whose bow was inscribed its name...

...*True Love.*

The Pastèque Kingdom

IN THE PASTÈQUE Kingdom, there was nothing people liked more than melons.

They ate them for breakfast, for lunch, and for dinner. Birthdays were celebrated with melons, as were weddings and births. Even funerals were marked with a feasting of the precious fruit.

The only melons eaten were a striped variety, as only they grew in the dark, steep-sided valley in which the kingdom lay.

One day, a young man called Wilbur Melonius fell in love with a girl named Esmeralda, with eyes as green as the melons that she, and everyone else, so adored.

Getting down on bended knee, Wilbur asked her to marry him.

Esmeralda thought for a moment, then replied:

'If you love me so much, dear Wilbur, prove your love.'

'How shall I do that?' he asked, blank faced.

'By finding me something no one's ever known before.'

'What kind of thing, dearest?'

Esmeralda narrowed her eyes, sniffed, and said:

'A delicious new variety of melon.'

'But, dearest...'

'I have spoken,' Esmeralda said. 'If you return with a delicious new variety of melon, I shall marry you... and if you do not return with one, I'll never speak to you again.'

'Return from where, my love?'

'From your adventure.'

With that, Esmeralda turned round and strolled back into her house, slamming the door behind her. Wilbur was left wondering where to go and what to do. He'd never left the kingdom before, and had no idea how to go about searching for anything, let alone a delicious new variety of melon.

But, being the resourceful young man he was, he climbed the path to the ruined castle at the top of the cliffs and sought out a wizard who resided there with his haggard old cat.

Explaining his predicament, he asked for advice.

'The solution is obvious,' the magician answered. 'Take to the road and don't return until you've found another kind of melon with which to impress your true love, Esmeralda.'

'But what if I don't find one?' he moaned.

'If that happens, you'll have to deal with it.'

So, Wilbur Melonius climbed down into the valley and set off on the road leading out of town – a road he'd never ventured upon until that very day.

After a few hours of trudging, Wilbur came to the border, where the Pastèque Kingdom ended and the Land of Blinding-Red Carrots began. Without giving it much thought, the young adventurer traversed the no man's land, and walked on.

Although anxious at travelling alone in a realm that was unfamiliar, something goaded him on, as though it was his destiny to make the journey in exactly the way he was making it.

From time to time he would pass fields in valleys between the mountains. But unlike in his own kingdom, the farmers were not growing melons, but abundant crops of bright-red carrots.

Pausing for the night at a caravanserai, he went in search of food.

In a small teahouse on the edge of the encampment, he asked for a slice of watermelon with which to refresh himself.

'We don't have melons here,' said the owner. 'All we have are blinding-red carrots. There's carrot stew, carrot soup, and carrot dumplings.'

Wilbur gobbled down a bowl of hot carrot soup, and was thankful for it. But, despite pretending to like it, he was already missing the taste of melons.

Next day, he continued, covering half the kingdom at a punishing pace. From time to time he came upon a local crofter, each one of whom was growing blinding-red carrots. When he asked if they ever grew melons, the farmers shook their heads from side to side and pointed to the fields of carrots.

Disheartened, Wilbur strode on, crossing the no man's land into the next country – the Kingdom of Enormous Aubergines. From the first moment he set foot there, he grasped that melons would be hard, if not impossible, to find.

Piled up beside the border post were crates of plump aubergines, going for export to a kingdom far away. The fields were lined with impressive aubergine plants, and the caravanserai teahouses were awash with succulent dishes made from the vegetables – roasted aubergines, stuffed aubergines, and baba ghanoush.

After picking his way through an aubergine fritter, Wilbur got chatting to one of the locals.

'I'm searching for a new kind of melon,' he explained. 'D'you know where I might find one?'

The local scratched his head.

'This is the Kingdom of Enormous Aubergines,' he replied, 'so we don't eat melons. But you could try the next kingdom, or the one after that.'

The following morning, Wilbur Melonius set off before dawn, crossing into the Land of Fried Eggs.

The ground there was rocky and, as the name would suggest, the farmers tended to rear chickens for eggs, which were fried for breakfast, lunch, and dinner.

Without bothering to pause, the young adventurer carried on, until he reached the neighbouring country, the Kingdom of Gleaming Pumpkins.

As soon as he'd crossed the no man's land and spotted the orderly rows of orange fruit laid out in the fields, Wilbur's heart sank once again. At this rate he'd never find a delicious new kind of melon with which to win his beloved Esmeralda's heart.

He was about to march on to the next kingdom, when something caused him to pause at the edge of a rocky little field.

An aged farmer was moaning to his wife:

'I have no idea what happened,' he said, 'but the seeds I was sold were fakes. Instead of being a wonderful new variety of delicious yellow-skinned pumpkins, they've turned out to be melons.'

The farmer's wife broke down in tears.

'We'll be ruined,' she said. 'For no one in the Kingdom of Gleaming Pumpkins has a taste for melons.'

Having overheard the conversation, Wilbur stepped forward.

'Could I taste one of your melons?' he asked.

'Go ahead,' the farmer answered, 'but don't blame me if you think they taste absolutely foul.'

Taking out his pocketknife, Wilbur cut one of the melons open.

Marvelling at the fine lime-green flesh inside, he took a bite.

It was the most delicious thing he'd ever tasted.

His heart racing, he said:

'I am a poor wayfarer on my travels from far away. As such, I don't have much money. But if you were to trust me, and transport this crop of yellow melons back to my kingdom, I promise you'll sell them for a considerably high price.'

The farmer had never been out of the kingdom before, but the prospect of making a fortune excited him.

'If we made money, we could retire!' he whispered.

And so the farmer agreed.

The next day he piled his cart with the yellow melons, then he and Wilbur set off for the Pastèque Kingdom.

They travelled for days on end, from the Kingdom of Gleaming Pumpkins, back through the Land of Fried Eggs and the Kingdom of Enormous Aubergines, and the Land of Blinding-Red Carrots.

Eventually, weary and tired, they traversed the no man's land to the kingdom where Wilbur Melonius was from.

Heading straight for Esmeralda's home, the young adventurer smartened himself up, rapped on the front door, and got down on one knee, a perfect yellow melon in his hands.

'My beloved,' he said, 'I have journeyed to the farthest land imaginable, and have brought back a new variety of melon with which to secure your heart.'

Esmeralda raised an eyebrow.

'Well, it certainly looks different to the melons we all know and love,' she said, 'but how does it taste?'

Pulling out his pocketknife, Wilbur cut a slice and served it.

A moment later, the face of his beloved was glinting with delight.

'This is the most mouth-tingling melon I've ever tasted!' she cried.

'So, will you marry me, dearest Esmeralda?'

'Yes, yes, yes, I will!'

News of the young adventurer's return and his betrothal spread at lightning speed. Everyone had heard of the rare and delicious yellow melons, and wanted to taste one for themselves.

And, very soon, they had.

Within an hour of setting up a stall in the town square, the farmer from the Kingdom of Gleaming Pumpkins had sold out. Thanking Wilbur, he set off for home, a bag of gold tucked into the folds of his robe.

Day and night, the people from the Pastèque Kingdom feasted on the amazing new melons. All they did was talk about them, delighting in their beauty and their taste. As the one who'd brought them back from his travels, they were called 'Wilbur melons'.

The farmers tore up their crops of watermelons and sowed the seeds of the new fruit. Very soon, carts of the bright-yellow Wilbur melons were being ferried to the market, where they replaced the standard watermelons overnight.

Within a few weeks, the yellow melons had completely replaced the watermelons which, until then, everyone had loved and enjoyed.

By royal decree, the Pastèque Kingdom was renamed the Land of the Wilbur Melon. The mere mention of a watermelon singled someone out as old-fashioned and passé. Yellow melons were heralded as the finest and most delectable fruits in existence.

Overnight, special pageants were devised to show them off, and competitions were established in which the very best-shaped Wilbur melons were given awards.

Wilbur and Esmeralda were married, and everyone in the Land of the Wilbur Melon rejoiced.

Time passed.

Then, one day, an old crone in the market was heard to say:

'I wish they still sold watermelons, like the ones we used to have.'

At first, the old woman was mocked and shooed away.

But, then, another crone spoke out…

'The lovely old watermelons quenched my thirst more than the Wilbur melons.'

And someone else added:

'I miss them too. Eating them reminded me of my childhood.'

'Wilbur melons give me stomach aches,' another woman moaned. 'I don't like them any more.'

All of a sudden, people throughout the kingdom were crying out for the old watermelons.

A royal adviser rushed into the throne room.

'Your Majesty!' he yelled. 'There's about to be a public revolt!'

The monarch listened, and was told that, although the yellow melons had not changed in any way, everyone was denouncing them – just as they had denounced the watermelons a few weeks before.

'Tell the farmers to sow their fields with watermelon seeds,' he groaned.

'But what shall we do with all the Wilbur melons that have been grown?'

'Have them taken to the end of the kingdom and thrown over the cliff into the sea.'

Wincing, the chief adviser scratched a thumb to his nose.

'What of the name of our kingdom, sire?'

The monarch groaned a second time.

'Have it changed back to the Pastèque Kingdom,' he said.

And so it came to pass that the yellow melons were banished, even though they themselves were not at fault at all. Merely mentioning them by name was decreed illegal. The very same watermelons that everyone had always known and loved were grown once again.

As for Wilbur Melonius, he went on to raise a large family with his beloved Esmeralda.

A century and a half slipped by.

Then, one day, a descendant of Wilbur Melonius fell in love with a girl. She had lovely flaxen hair and dimples in her cheeks.

'I'll marry you,' she said, 'if you venture far away and bring something for me.'

The young man looked into his true love's eyes.

'Anything at all,' he answered. 'Anything between here and the sun.'

The girl grinned.

'When I was a child, I heard a fairy tale,' she said. 'It was about a special kind of yellow melon – a melon that was loved by one and all, and was then hated as much as it had been loved.'

The young man frowned.

'Yes, I remember hearing the story before bed.'

'Bring me one of the yellow melons,' said the girl, 'or else I will never speak to you again.'

So, next morning, the young man set off for the Land of Blinding-Red Carrots. In the grand adventure that followed, he brought back a cart of yellow melons, and the cycle of love and loathing began all over again…

Just as it had in the age of Wilbur Melonius long, long before.

Sherlock Melon

In the Land of the Delectable Melons, a killer was on the loose.

He'd struck three times already, leaving fear in his wake, and turning the sleepy little country upside down.

An elderly grandmother melon had been chopped in two while out at the shops.

A postman melon had been poisoned.

And a farmer had been butchered in his sleep.

All three victims bore the now familiar calling card of the assassin:

The shape of a melon seed carved into their backs.

Fearful the public would turn against him, the mayor went on Melonvision and pleaded for calm.

'We'll catch the killer!' he exclaimed. 'I promise we'll catch him within a week!'

As the lights dimmed, the mayor's chief adviser looked fraught.

'How are you planning to catch him?' he asked.

Straightening his back, the mayor was stern.

'My job as a politician is to make promises,' he said gruffly. 'Your job is to keep the promises that I make!'

The chief adviser went home to his wife and poured himself a big glass of melon fizz.

'If we don't catch the killer, the public will be up in arms!' he cried. 'Worse still, the mayor will lose his backing from Melon K. Melon, proprietor of *The Melon Gazette*, and owner of Melonvision as well. But, worst of all, I will lose my job!'

'Why don't you ask the Melon Detective to solve the case?' lisped the chief adviser's wife.

'Who's he?'

'The cleverest melon who ever lived, that's who!'

'Where would I find him?'

'At the south end of town. They say he's so clever that he can solve the unsolvable.'

Next morning, the mayor's chief adviser went to the south end of town. After asking directions from more than a dozen melons, he came to a little house painted green and red.

A prim brass plaque screwed to the door read:

Sherlock Melon
Consulting Detective

The adviser soon found himself face to face with Sherlock Melon, and wasted no time in explaining what was known so far.

Nodding studiously, the consulting detective leaned back in his favourite chair, drew on his pipe, and said:

'There's nothing quite so satisfying as a serial melon killer on the loose.'

The mayor's chief adviser balked.

'Please find the assassin,' he said, 'for all our sakes.'

'I'll do it on one condition,' Sherlock Melon replied.

'Anything. Name your price!'

'When I catch the assassin, you must allow me to make the announcement live on Melonvision.'

The chief adviser to the mayor agreed, and next morning Sherlock Melon got on the case.

Through days and nights, the detective crisscrossed the Land of Delectable Melons on the trail of clues.

A consummate master of disguise, he blended in wherever he went, recording a list of relevant details in the little black notebook hanging in a pouch on his belt. Naturally, everyone who saw him merely assumed he was a member of the public – that is, if they saw him at all.

First, he popped up at a tea party for elderly ladies, widowed by the Great Melon War. In the guise of an heiress named Tabitha Honeydew, wearing a bright sequinned gown and a string of pearls around his neck, he explained how horrified he'd been to hear that an elderly grandmother just like him had been cleaved in two by the killer.

After that, the melon detective appeared as a parcel, all wrapped up in brown paper and string, collected from Melon Hall, and delivered to the Melon Docks.

Next, he was standing in a field, dressed as a melon scarecrow, tufts of straw and ragged clothing as his disguise.

With pressure growing on the mayor to catch the killer, he went on Melonvision yet again, and announced:

'Fear not, dear voters, I have engaged the services of the greatest detective who's ever lived – Sherlock Melon! We will have the assassin behind bars by the end of the week!'

But, an hour after the mayor's address, the melon killer struck again.

This time, the victim was a tourist from another country, exploring the Land of Delectable Melon's historic sites with her husband.

As before, the shape of a melon seed had been scored deep into her back.

The day after that, a famous melon soprano collapsed on stage at the Melon Opera, the very same melon seed proof that it was the serial killer's work.

Sherlock Melon worked round the clock, visiting relevant sites, taking samples, and interviewing witnesses, without them realizing they were being interviewed at all.

Sales of *The Melon Gazette* soared as the public clamoured for up-to-date information on the case. The tabloid published witness accounts, timelines and graphs, leader columns, sketches, profiles, and endless hypotheses.

All the while, Sherlock Melon continued his investigation.

He took samples of dirt from the melon tourist's shoes, and noted down the perfume worn by the celebrated soprano. He listened to the cows in the murdered farmer's field as they grazed and gossiped, as cows tend to do. And he even posed as a journalist in the editorial offices of *The Melon Gazette*.

That night, as the melon detective crawled into bed, he got a tipoff from one of his sources. The killer had claimed his sixth victim – a clown called Melony-Moo.

The entire Land of Delectable Melons went into hysteria at the news. After all, the veteran entertainer was a national treasure, a figure more loved than anyone else.

A state funeral was laid on for Melony-Moo, the most intricate details of which were covered by *The Melon Gazette*.

Everyone in the Land of Delectable Melons put on their finest clothing and turned out to applaud the hearse as it zigzagged through the streets – a last chance to honour the celebrated clown, Melony-Moo.

The only person missing was Sherlock Melon.

Under deep cover, he made appearances in a hundred guises, although no one ever guessed it was him.

Six days and nights after being hired by the mayor, the great melon detective sent a message to city hall. It read:

Prepare the Melonvision studio for eight p.m. this evening STOP

The killer will be unmasked live on air STOP

The detective's message was hurried up to the mayor's office. Ten minutes later, news of the intended unmasking had been broadcast over the airwaves in the Land of Delectable Melons, and far beyond.

That evening, Sherlock Melon put on his best suit and travelled from the south end of town to the Melonvision studios, where he was greeted by Melon K. Melon, the mayor, and an abundance of fawning minions.

'Are you certain you know the identity of the killer?' the mayor growled.

'Of course I do,' Sherlock Melon responded. 'But please remember – the truth is sometimes not the truth one might wish for.'

A dab of makeup was smudged over the melon detective's bald head, and he was led into the studio. The bright lights came on, then a countdown...

Four...

Three...

Two...

One...

Poised before the camera, Sherlock Melon was calm and collected.

'My dear friends in the Land of Delectable Melons, I am pleased to say that I have identified the killer, and will reveal his identity in a moment. But first I would like to explain the sequence of events, of clues in this most revealing of cases.

'Everyone, it seems, has an opinion on who the assassin might be, and so I should like to explain something right at the start. It is this: there is not one assassin, but *six* of them.'

A communal surge of excited expectation tore through the land.

'My God,' said the mayor, standing in the wings.

'Great for ratings!' hissed Melon K. Melon under his breath.

Taking a sip of water, the detective continued:

'The first victim, the grandmother melon, who was chopped in two so brutally, was in actual fact killed by the melon postman, who was to become the second casualty in the case. The postman melon was in turn poisoned by the farmer melon, who was himself hacked into pieces by a very sharp knife. This is where things get even more interesting,' Sherlock Melon declared. 'You see, it was none other than the soprano melon who killed the farmer, and the tourist who in turn killed her. And, as you may have now deduced for yourselves, it was indeed the clown, our beloved Melony-Moo, who took the life of the tourist.'

Watching in amazement on giant screens in town squares, in taverns, and homes, the people of the Land of Delectable Melons could hardly believe what they were hearing.

His expression composed, the great melon detective pressed his hands together and looked straight into the camera.

'Two questions remain unanswered,' he said. 'First: who killed Melony-Moo? And second: why did these murders take place?'

Getting to his feet, Sherlock Melon strode purposefully towards the camera.

'There's something more important to consider, however,' he said. 'It's that the truth can be viewed in different ways.'

'What's he getting at?' the mayor hissed to his chief adviser, standing beside him in the wings.

The melon detective raised a forefinger.

'And in this case, the truth is not only unlikely, but it is one I venture that no one watching would have fathomed. You see, while it appears that our case has six victims, in actual fact it has none at all. The grandmother, the postman, the farmer, soprano, tourist, and our beloved Melony-Moo are all alive and well.'

A communal gasp tore through the Land of Delectable Melons.

When it had died down, Sherlock Melon clapped his hands.

To the delight of the audience, all six victims stepped forward from the darkness.

Reeling from shock, the mayor strained to work out what was going on.

The detective called for hush.

'The murders – or rather, the *would-be* murders – were nothing more than a ruse,' he explained. 'A ruse contrived by Melon K. Melon in the name of increasing the circulation of his *Gazette*, and audience figures for Melonvision.'

Sherlock Melon beckoned for the station's proprietor to join him on the stage.

Awkwardly, Melon K. Melon stepped from the wings.

Tumultuous applause followed.

The melon detective smiled.

'We melons are curious things,' he said. 'There's nothing that excites us more than the prospect of murder, although at the same time there's nothing that repels us more than a murder. It appears that everyone was a winner: Melon K. Melon has boosted his ratings, and you the audience were entertained. My celebrity has surely increased. But best of all, no melons – innocent or otherwise – were harmed.'

The Fox, the Dog, and the River's Soul

Once upon a time, long ago in a far-off land, there lived a fox and a dog.

Although dogs and foxes are sometimes regarded as rivals, this dog and this fox were best friends.

They'd been reared together, and had spent their young months playing down at the river's bend, splashing and laughing through the warm days at the end of summer.

In the land where they lived, foxes and dogs tended not to be given names. So we shall call the fox 'Fox', and we shall call the dog 'Dog'.

One day Fox said to the dog:

'Let's go on a journey.'

Dog replied:

'A journey to where?'

'To the source of the river,' said Fox.

Dog pricked up his ears.

'And what do you expect us to find there?'

'Our fortunes,' Fox said.

So, early next morning, Fox and Dog set off along the riverbank in search of their fortunes.

They hadn't gone far when they came to a cow, grazing at the water's edge on lush green grass.

'Hello cow,' they said.

Returning the greeting, the cow asked:

'If you don't mind me asking, where would a fox and a dog be going together?'

'We're in search of the end of the river,' Dog said.

'And in search of our fortunes,' Fox chipped in.

'Well,' answered the cow, 'as I am old and wise, and as you are both so foolish and young, I shall give you some advice. It's never wise to cross the river in the light of a full moon.'

'Why?' asked Fox.

'Because,' the cow replied, 'that's when the river serpent lies beneath the surface, waiting to feast on nice young dogs, and nice young foxes, like the both of you.'

Thanking the cow, the pair of adventurers continued towards the river's source.

They walked all day, until the pads of their feet were sore and their backs were hot from the sun.

In the afternoon, they caught a pair of big, fat fish and gobbled them up, thanking providence for having made them the wily young hunters they were.

When the shadows were long and the birds were nesting in the willow trees, the dog and the fox curled up on the riverbank and fell asleep.

Next morning, when they awoke, the sun was already high.

'We'd better get moving,' said Fox. 'For there is a lot of riverbank still to cover.'

Yawning long and hard, Dog said:

'Last night I dreamed we reached the source of the river, and we were crowned kings.'

The fox smiled, but secretly he thought it was a silly dream – the kind dogs have, but which foxes regard as nonsense.

All through the day they walked, until again the shadows were long.

When they were weary, they again caught big, fat fish and feasted.

Just before they curled up to sleep, they heard a grandmother owl hooting in the willow tree above them.

'Hello dog and hello fox,' she hooted.

The travellers returned the pleasantries.

'What brings you to these parts?' asked the owl.

'We're going in search of the river's source,' said the dog.

'And to find our fortunes,' the fox added.

'I am old and not long for this world,' the owl

said, 'but in my youth I flew far to the north, and I spied the beginning of the river.'

'Really?' cried the dog boisterously.

'What was it like?' asked the fox.

The owl let out a long, fearful hoot.

'It was not as I expected it to be,' she said.

'D'you have any advice for a fox and a dog in search of the river's source?' asked the dog.

Again, the grandmother owl hooted. And, ruffling up her feathers, she answered:

'Even though your journey may be a long one, don't question it. Keep going despite the difficulties, or whatever gets in the way.'

Thanking the wise owl, the dog and the fox fell fast asleep.

When they woke next morning, there was no sign of the grandmother bird.

'I'm worrying we will never find our way back to the bend in the river from where we started,' said Dog, as they walked along.

'What does it matter?' asked Fox. 'We can simply live on another river bend.'

'But I have brothers and sisters, and a mother and a father,' the dog replied. 'They will miss me, and I will miss them.'

'Well, think how proud of you they'll be once you return from the source of the river,' Fox said. 'They'll lick you all over and tell you how wonderful you are.'

'Yes,' said Dog, feeling warm inside, 'you're right. They'll lick me all over and I shall like that very much indeed.'

All through the day they walked.

Sometimes the riverbank was shaded by willow trees, and at other times it was rocky and barren.

Sometimes the water was smooth as silk, and at other times it was a swirling rumpus of rapids and rocks.

Day after day, Dog and Fox walked.

And day after day, they wondered what they would find at the source, and whether it would have been worth it.

A full week after setting out from the bend in the river, they came to a mother rabbit. She was sitting on a little mound overlooking the river, and appeared alarmed at spotting the adventurers.

'Don't worry,' Fox called out. 'We're not going to eat you because we're in a hurry.'

'And in any case,' said Dog, 'we've got used to eating the big, fat fish in the river.'

'Pleased to hear it,' the rabbit replied. 'In return for sparing me, let me tell you this: if you keep going up the riverbank you'll come to a castle in which there lives a cruel hunter. He garnished my entire family with garlic, then gobbled them up, and he happens to dislike dogs and foxes very greatly indeed.'

'Oh,' said the dog.

'Oh,' said the fox.

The rabbit twitched her nose and said:

'If you come across the hunter, simply warn him that you're in the lead of an invading army, and that he ought to hurry to his castle and lock himself inside.'

Thanking the mother rabbit, the dog and the fox carried on.

Late next morning, they came upon the castle in which the cruel hunter lived.

As they crept past its south wall, they heard the sound of feet behind them.

Both turned at once.

The cruel hunter was standing ten feet away, a shotgun balanced between his hands.

'Give me one good reason not to kill you both,' he snarled.

'Because behind us is a vast army,' said Fox.

'And if you shoot us,' Dog added, 'our masters will tear you limb from limb.'

The cruel hunter looked very worried.

'*Whhhhat* shall I do?' he stammered.

'Hurry to your castle, bolt the doors and shutter the windows!' cried Dog.

And that is exactly what the hunter did.

Through days and weeks, the fox and the dog continued on their journey, following the twists and turns of the river.

When the wind was strong and the rain was cold, they wondered why they were adventuring at all.

Sometimes Dog would whinge that they should go back, but Fox would rally his spirits. And, at other times, one or the other would moan, claiming their paws hurt.

But the wise owl's advice, to keep going at all costs, echoed in their ears.

Days became weeks, weeks became months, and the pair of travellers found themselves at a cave perched at the water's edge. They both knew that venturing inside would put them at risk of being attacked by a bear.

For that reason they tiptoed past.

Just as they reached the far side of the cave, they heard not the ferocious growling of an enraged bear, but the calm voice of a kindly one.

Before they knew it, Dog and Fox had explained who they were, why they had come, and where they were going.

The bear, who was about to turn in for his long hibernation, wished the dog and the fox good travels.

Giving thanks, the fox asked whether the bear had any advice for them.

'Yes, I do,' he answered at once. 'It's this – when you finally get to the source of the river, look for the soul of the river, and take it home with you.'

'What will it be like?' asked the dog.

'All I can tell you is that it will be contained in two layers.'

'What kind of layers?'

'I can't say,' replied the bear. 'But you will know them when you find them.'

Wishing the bear well, they left him to his long hibernation, and continued for many more days.

And that's how the dog and the fox reached the final bend of the once-mighty river.

Having left the plain weeks before, they had traced the watercourse up into the mountains, where the air was chill and the landscape was barren.

With almost no life in a river so young, they were forced to spend more and more time searching for fish, and less and less time pressing ahead.

On the final night of their journey, the river was so slim that both Dog and Fox knew they were almost at the source. Their sense of anticipation was tempered by a fear of failure – failure at finding nothing, and being regarded as fools.

As the pair of travellers curled up for the night, they heard a chilling noise in the distance. It sounded like a herd of stampeding elephants.

'We must swim across the river!' said Fox urgently.

Dog pointed to the cloudless sky, in which a full moon was glinting.

'Remember what the old cow told us at the start of our journey, all those months ago?'

'That the river serpent would gobble us up were we to swim in the light of the full moon.'

The sound of stampeding elephants grew all the louder.

'We must swim for it or else we'll be trampled into the dust!' cried the dog.

The fox sniffed the air.

Unlike his companion, he was level-headed and calm.

'Both of us are blessed with certain senses,' he said, 'one of them being the ability to smell better than almost anything alive. So, tell me, can you smell a herd of elephants?'

His eyes wide with fear, Dog sniffed. Even though he was panicked, he had to admit he couldn't smell a single elephant, let alone a herd of them.

Fox cleared his throat.

'If this journey's taught me anything,' he said, 'it is not to rush to judgement. If you think back to all our adventures, we have survived by keeping a level head, even when in the face of terrible uncertainty.'

Dog thanked Fox.

Fox replied:

'Let's get up at dawn and make our way around the last bend, and see what awaits us.'

And that's what the fox and the dog did.

Long before the first rays of dazzling mountain light had broken over the horizon, the pair of travellers passed the final bend, and found themselves at a little pool of water.

Bubbling and gurgling, it was the source of the river, along which they had walked through weeks and months.

Beside it was a great mechanical digger, the likes of which neither Dog nor Fox had ever seen before. On its way to the nearby mine, it had been the cause of the tumultuous hullabaloo the evening before. But, having run out of fuel, its operator had made his way down to the village at the foot of the mountains.

The fox and the dog had no interest in the machine.

As far as they were concerned, it was one of many senseless contrivances conjured by mankind to do harm to the realm they shared with nature. But they both realized that had they swum the river the night before, they would have plunged to their deaths over a cliff.

Strolling over to the pool, they thanked providence once again for taking care of them on their long journey, and for providing them with such first-rate adventures.

'Pity there are no fish here,' said Dog, peering into the crystal water.

'You read my mind,' answered Fox.

'And it's a pity there's no hint of the river's soul,' said his companion.

The dog padded around the pool, marvelling at the way water was bubbling up from the ground. He was about to stretch out in the sun when he spotted something at the water's edge.

Round in shape, it was wrapped in a chequered red-and-white cloth.

Inquisitive by nature, Dog strode over and pulled the cloth away with his snout, revealing a large watermelon. The operator of the digger had planned to quench his thirst with it before the machine had broken down.

'Wonder what this is doing here,' said Fox.

Dog didn't reply at first. He was concentrating.

'Two layers,' he said.

'What?' asked the fox.

'The cloth and the juicy red flesh.'

'I don't understand what you mean,' said Fox.

Grasping the melon in his front paws, the dog threw it onto the ground, splitting it open.

'There!' he cried, motioning to the seeds. 'They are the river's soul – protected by the flesh, and by the cloth.'

Ravenous, Dog and Fox gobbled up all the melon, leaving only the rind and the seeds.

When they were refreshed, Fox gathered the seeds into the cloth. Dog tied it up, and they set off with it – with the melon's soul – retracing their steps.

Through weeks and months, they travelled home, the melon seeds guarded against rain, hail, and snow. And, eventually, they arrived back at the river bend from which they'd set out on that fine spring morning so many months before.

As soon as they arrived, Dog's brothers and sisters, mother and father, hurried over.

And a crowd gathered.

'Where have you been?' they all asked at once.

'To the source of the river.'

The creatures in attendance gasped in amazement. Some asked questions, while others tut-tutted as to why rash young dogs and foxes felt the need to go off in search of anything.

As the questions died down, an elderly otter asked what the pair had discovered at the source of the river.

'The river's soul,' said Fox.

Opening out the cloth, which was now blackened with dirt and mud, they showed off the seeds.

'Here it is,' said Dog.

'They look like melon seeds,' the otter said.

'Well,' answered the fox pointedly, 'what are we to do if the river's soul is made of melon seeds?'

As night drew near, the creatures left the riverbank, returning to their nests and their burrows.

Fox and Dog lived long, happy lives.

With time, their families told stories about them and their adventures...

Stories that are now told to every dog puppy and every fox cub along the river's great length.

Marsimus Melon

ONCE UPON A time, just beyond the next horizon, there lived a family of melons.

A father melon.

A mother melon.

And a teenage melon, named Marsimus.

Through a childhood spent playing in the fields and down where the river was wide, little Marsimus learned all the things which a melon would need to know for a good, honest life.

He learned how to read and write and count.

He learned how to help old lady melons across the street.

He learned how to be respectful to both strangers and friends.

And, most of all, he learned how to give more than he took.

One day, Marsimus was old enough to venture into the world.

Clustering around, his parents begged him to be careful. Then, they pointed to the sun setting at the far end of the field – the field in which Marsimus had been born.

'You must set off in search of your fame and fortune,' Father Melon said.

'And you must find your true love,' Mother Melon added.

Their son seemed fearful.

'But I have never been out of the village,' he said.

'Of course you haven't,' said Father Melon. 'And that's why you must go now.'

'But what if I meet bad people?' asked Marsimus.

'Well, then,' his mother intoned, 'simply be as kind to them as kind can be.'

At dawn next morning, the young melon hugged his father and his mother. And, with tears in his eyes, he set off towards the horizon, his feet dragging slowly from fear.

He walked, and he walked.

And he walked, and he walked.

Through fields and then across the great plains.

Through forests and then across the mountains.

Along the way he encountered rich melons and poor melons, kind melons and horrid melons. And, once in a while, he met a melon who gave him advice.

An old mother melon told him to keep out of the mud.

An old father melon told him to keep away from the beehives.

A wise witch melon told him to keep bad thoughts out of his head.

And a wise wizard melon told him to never look up into the night sky.

At that last advice, Marsimus shrugged.

'Of course I don't look up into the night sky,' he said.

'Why not?'

'Well, sir, like all us melons, I don't have a neck, so I can't throw my head back and look up at the sky.'

The wise wizard melon sniffed.

'You could look up at the sky when you lie on your back in bed,' he said curtly.

The young traveller shrugged again.

'I don't sleep on my back,' he said.

Through days and through weeks, Marsimus continued in search of his fame and fortune.

There were times when he was tired, but he kept on going.

And there were times when he missed his home and family, but still he carried on towards the next horizon.

One day he reached a chain of mountains, higher and bleaker than any mountains he had ever imagined. They looked as though someone had painted them slimy black with tar, and had then sprinkled them with talc.

As they were in the way of reaching the next horizon, young Marsimus climbed them, even though he wished he didn't have to.

Day after day he climbed.

Through the forest.

And through the ferns.

Up over the rocks and crags.

Across valleys as wide as any.

Until he reached the snowline.

Frozen to the bone, Marsimus trudged forwards, one frozen foot in front of the other.

As tears welled in his eyes and rolled down his cheeks, he begged the melon ancestors to transport him home to Mother Melon and Father Melon.

For a fraction of a second, he even contemplated turning around and heading back in the direction from which he had come.

His mind reeling from fatigue and from sorrow, he heard a sound that put the fear of the melon god into him.

The sound of the ice beneath him cracking and breaking.

Crack! Crack! Crack!

It was followed by the tumult of the young melon adventurer tumbling over.

A clamour not dissimilar to the terror and dread of the wicked melon ancestors, of whom melon mothers and fathers tell little melon children on dark winter nights.

A commotion that rang out from Marsimus's lips.

The clamour ended when, with a thump, the young adventurer found himself lying on his back for the first time in his life.

Entombed in snow and ice, he lay there, his mind as calm as calm can be.

Eyes staring straight up, breathing slowed, it was

as though every footstep of his great journey had been in preparation for that moment.

A moment as tranquil as it was perfect.

Marsimus's eyes drank in the last strains of afternoon light, feeling the warmth on his mottled green skin.

As he lay there, exhausted and in awe, he watched as the nocturnal firmament was revealed.

One at a time, and then in twos, and threes, the stars began to glint.

Flickering into life, they covered every square inch of the mesmerizing starscape.

As he watched, transfixed, a great ivory-white ball of light was projected onto the stage of darkness.

An ivory-white ball, the likes of which he had never seen, let alone imagined.

More lovely than the most serene memory on an ancient's lips, it seemed to twinkle like a gemstone in a treasure trove.

All of a sudden, young Marsimus understood that he had discovered the one thing he was destined to discover – the thing that had required an epic adventure to locate.

His lips pursed as though summoning the courage to address an empress, Marsimus whispered:

'I have crossed mountains, deserts, and forests, and have trudged to all points of the compass, just so that I might see you now, and in this special place.'

Nestled in the heavens far above, the full moon glistened and gleamed, as though pleased by the words of the traveller.

She glistened and gleamed, but she did not respond in spoken words.

Undeterred, the young melon adventurer blew a kiss to the great ball of ivory.

A kiss of longing and of love.

'Now that I've seen you here, above this great mountain, I am content to return to the place where

I am from. By setting eyes upon you, my life and its mission has changed. I feel as though I have purpose.'

As before, the moon seemed to listen.

But, once again, she remained silent.

Blowing another kiss, and weeping a tear of unspoken reflection, Marsimus melon clambered out of the snow and ice, and headed for home.

Mazubicam and the
Melon Treasure

Once upon a time in a certain place, there was a kingdom in the shadow of the mountains.

In this kingdom was a farm, and on the farm were a few goats and chickens. Tending them was a little boy named Julius. His father having died when he was small, the child had no choice but to look after the goats so that his grandmother, with whom he lived, could sell goat cheese and fresh eggs down in the market.

Nothing of much interest ever happened on the farm.

Julius would spend his days roaming the hillside crags, wondering what it would be like to go to school, to travel, or to have a different kind of life than he did.

One day, while following the goats as they ambled

towards the shade, he noticed something sticking out of the ground.

A hook made from a twisted loop of rusted iron.

Intrigued, Julius stooped down and tugged at the hook.

He pulled and he pulled…

And he pulled and he pulled…

But the rusted iron hook didn't budge.

He was about to give up and go tend the goats when a voice in his head whispered:

'Julius, take off your belt. Thread it through the twisted iron loop and pull with all your might.'

Doing as the voice had bid him, the goatherd pulled and pulled.

And, to his delight, the rock in which the hook was embedded moved to the side.

Below, a cavern was revealed.

Fearing what his grandmother would say were she to find out, he pushed the rock back into place and hurried over to the goats.

All through the blistering afternoon, however, the goatherd couldn't think of anything but the cave he'd discovered.

However hard he tried to put it out of his mind, it kept slipping back. Until, unable to stand it any longer, he waited until the flock was grazing and crept over to the rock.

Pushing it away again, he peered into the cavern.

To his surprise, he saw a flight of steps leading down.

Led by curiosity, Julius climbed down onto the first step and descended into the chamber, which appeared to be illuminated by shafts of natural light.

Never in his wildest dreams had the goatherd ever imagined what he found inside.

The cavern was a treasure vault, packed floor to ceiling with a king's ransom of riches: enormous sculptures, vast platters, sacks of coins – all crafted from the finest gold.

In pride of place at the middle of it all was an object that almost defied description – a magnificent solid-gold throne in the shape of a melon. Adorning its surface, the history of a kingdom was inscribed – a kingdom long since reduced to dust.

Approaching, Julius did his best to make out the tale – an epic of trial and tribulation, conquest and woe. On the arms of the golden melon throne was a pair of couplets.

His finger tracing the words, Julius read them:

In deeds and good the Melon King
Ruled in awe and joy and angels sing;
He who defends the glory of this throne
Shall summon the wonder of Mazubicam!

As the last word left the goatherd's lips, the cavern began to shake, the ground quaking.

A blinding flash of light, and a jinn appeared.

Arms crossed, a golden turban crowning his head, he appeared both surprised and furious to have been woken from his slumber.

'Who wakes Mazubicam?' he bellowed.

Cowering, Julius didn't dare speak.

But the jinn cried out again.

'Forgive me, O great spirit,' the boy stammered. 'It was *I*, a humble goatherd.'

As though struggling to focus on a grain of dust, the jinn peered down.

'What do you have to say before I devour you, O insignificant wretch of humanity?'

Terrified, Julius was about to plead for mercy when he remembered something – something his grandmother had once told him: 'Never forget that jinns appear imposing, but they're very foolish under the surface.'

So, even though he was trembling, the goatherd replied:

'O Great Mazubicam! You tower as high as a mighty tree, and your voice booms like a thousand ogres, but I am sure you are not as high and mighty as you appear!'

On hearing the goatherd's words, the jinn shook from head to toe, his colossal form swelling to double its original size.

Clenching a fist, he prepared to dispatch the boy with a single blow.

But just as he was about to strike, Julius spoke again.

'I'll tell you a secret!' he yelled.

Grunting with displeasure, Mazubicam paused.

'I have no need of a secret spoken from the lips of such an insignificant creature as you!'

'How do you know?' the goatherd responded fast.

'Because you're a human, and I am a jinn!'

'*So*?'

Mazubicam rolled his eyes.

'Everyone knows that humans are the most good-for-nothing species of creature ever to have graced the heavens or the earth!'

'It's a really good secret,' Julius cried. 'Kill me and you'll find yourself wondering what it was!'

Again, the jinn rolled his eyes. Then he sighed.

'All right! Tell it to me, so I can get on with pounding you into paste!'

The goatherd thought back to all the hours of sitting on his grandmother's knee, for she was always spouting on about jinns. He remembered her describing the very best way to trick a jinn.

Cupping his hands around his mouth, Julius whispered in Mazubicam's direction.

'I can't hear you!' the jinn boomed.

'Then get down on your knees so that your ear is closer to my mouth,' the goatherd called out.

Curious as to what the secret might be, the jinn did as was bid of him, and got down on his knees.

Julius asked the jinn to lie down on the ground, as he still towered well above the height of a man.

The creature was losing patience, but the goatherd reminded him that the secret was most excellent.

Huffing and puffing, Mazubicam lay down on the ground.

Julius stepped forwards, a knotted kerchief in his hand. The knot, used against jinns by sorcerers for centuries, had been passed on to the boy while he was sitting on his grandmother's knee.

As soon as Mazubicam was lying outstretched, the goatherd leapt forwards, and thrust the knotted handkerchief into his ear.

Instantly, the creature fell under the boy's control.

'In the name of the forces of light and dark, I curse you!' cried the jinn, having realized what had taken place.

Julius strode over to the golden melon throne and sat upon it.

'O wretched Mazubicam! I order you to transport this throne to a desert far away!'

In the blink of an eye, the melon throne was transported to a sea of sand, the jinn crouching beside it on all fours.

Again, the boy spoke:

'O wretched Mazubicam! I command you to turn the desert into a fertile crescent, with rivers and palms, green fields, and with mountains touched with snow!'

In the blink of an eye, the desert had been transformed into the most fertile valley imaginable, with a line of serene, snow-capped mountains in the distance.

Breathing a sigh of pleasure, the goatherd spoke again:

'O wretched Mazubicam! I command you to build a palace worthy of this wondrous melon throne!'

In the blink of an eye, unseen hands constructed a golden palace. More lovely than any palace ever viewed by the eyes of man, it was built in the shape of a melon.

No sooner had the melon palace been materialized than something most curious occurred.

The great jinn Mazubicam called to the former goatherd, who was inside the palace, seated on the melon throne.

'Come out to the palace gardens,' he bawled, 'for there is something of concern in the distance!'

Julius clambered off the melon throne, strode down the long corridors, and out through the doors of the great melon palace.

Following the line of the jinn's outstretched arm, he peered at the horizon, a hand shading his eyes.

Far away, where the sky met the land, a ball was glistening.

'What is it?' the boy asked.

'A reaction,' answered Mazubicam.

'What do you mean – a *reaction*?'

The jinn sniffed.

'You may know how to trick us with a knotted kerchief,' he said, 'but it appears you don't know what happens when our powers are used for selfish reasons.'

Julius frowned.

'What happens?' he asked.

'A reaction, that's what.'

As Mazubicam explained, every action in the universe has a reaction – none more so than jinn magic. As the former goatherd was to learn, supernatural forces led to a disturbance in time and space, and an effect rather like the swinging of a pendulum.

'What's the glistening ball on the horizon all about?' he asked at length.

'It's biding its time,' said Mazubicam.

'Biding its time for what?'

'Biding its time until you are fast asleep. When you are, it'll race over the plain and will flatten your lovely melon palace, and everything else.'

'That's nonsense,' said Julius. 'My grandmother told me everything there is to know about jinns, and never once did she speak of a reaction.'

Mazubicam grunted once, and then again.

'That's because it's a secret,' he said.

The boy squinted at the glistening ball.

'Why are you telling me this?' he asked. 'Surely you would be quite happy for me to be flattened by whatever that is out there.'

The jinn grunted a third time.

'Unfortunately, being the jinn of the melon throne as I am, the reaction will take me down with it when it strikes.'

'So what do we do?' asked Julius.

'We strip the melon palace of its selfishness,' said Mazubicam. 'Only then will we be protected from the reaction taking place.'

Again, the boy who had until recently been a goatherd frowned.

His brow furrowed like a spring field. As it did so, he had an idea.

'O good Mazubicam!' he cried. 'I command you to transport to this citadel every sick and ailing soul from fifty horizons, and give them treatment and tenderness as they have never known!'

No sooner had the command left the boy's mouth than the melon palace was transformed into a melon hospital. The courtyards and the gardens, the apartments and the throne room itself were all filled with the infirm and with a legion of medical staff.

Gazing out at the distance, to where the sky met the land, Julius saw that the glistening ball had melted away. He walked through the palace and its gardens, surveying all the good that was being done.

Mazubicam sat in a nearby orchard, waiting for instructions. Julius found him there at the end of the day.

'First, I command you to transport all the golden treasure from the cavern, and sell it along with the melon throne. Have the proceeds invested, so that the melon hospital is secured for an eternity.'

The jinn blinked.

'It has been done,' he said.

Julius smiled.

'Very good,' he replied. 'Now, transport me back to my family's flock.'

Instantly, the boy was back in his own kingdom.

Beckoning Mazubicam to bend down, the goatherd reached into the jinn's ear and pulled out the knotted kerchief.

'Welcome to your freedom,' he said.

And with that, Julius the goatherd returned to his flock, his adventures at an end.

The Melon Mountain and the Valiant Ant

ONCE UPON A time there was a vast plain of empty land, known by the ants who lived there as 'the Bigness'.

Such was the size and scale of the landscape that none of the ants had ever crossed it from one end to the other.

Once in a while, an intrepid young ant would set off to go all the way to the end of the Bigness and back.

But the ants that set out in search of answers rarely returned.

Most of the ant population never thought to question the fact that the landscape was absolutely flat, hard as a rock, and empty. They lived in a nest under the ground, and would emerge to the surface in order to fetch the giant berries which were blown onto the plain by the breeze.

And, although none of the ants had ever ventured to the end of the Bigness and back again, the community's folklore was well developed.

Every young ant was weaned on a myth.

A myth which said that the flat, desolate plain had been created in ancient times by a fallen star – a fallen star in search of lost love. She had risked everything in order to discover the destiny which, she believed, was awaiting her.

At the end of the epic myth was a sentence known to every ant, whether it be a woman, a man, or a child:

'In the fullness of time and space, a vast and mystifying mountain shall appear, and shall give purpose to one and all.'

Time passed in the land of the ants.

One generation grew up, lived, thrived, passed on the myth, and faded away.

Again.

And again.

And again.

And a thousand more agains.

Nothing ever seemed to happen in the land of the ants – nothing that could be described as an unusual event.

But, one winter day, the wind whipped up more ferociously than usual, and blustered in from the south over the vast, desolate plain.

Hiding beneath the surface in their nest, the ants heard the wind and the rain – surging, churning, and clattering as though the end of time was about to befall them.

The young ants were fearful. But the seasoned old ants calmed them by telling the epic myth of the fallen star and her search for lost love.

All the while, the wind howled and the rain cascaded down.

In all the commotion of nature, a striped green melon was blown in from the farmer's field.

Tumbling in fits and jerks over the desolate plain, it came to a rest inches away from the entrance to the ants' nest.

And there it lay.

With time, the wind died down, and the rain gave way to sunshine.

The ants emerged from their nest and thanked the universe for sparing them from the ravages of the storm.

A few of the ants went about their business, gathering the berries which were fifty times their size.

All of a sudden, one of the ants yelled to the others.

'A mountain! A mountain! A mountain has appeared!'

In less time than it takes to tell, the ant population streamed out of the nest and clustered around.

'It is the mountain from the great ant epic!' they cried, voices united as one.

The excitement rose to a crescendo, and then died down.

Then, after an eternity of silence, a young ant said:

'What's the mountain for?'

No sooner had the question been spoken than another ant – a far more aged one – answered it:

'The mountain is to be climbed, that's what it's for!'

'But who will climb the mountain?' asked a boy ant.

Another eternity of silence came and went.

And a tender young girl ant answered:

'*I* shall climb it. I will climb the great green mountain that's appeared.'

And so it was that the brave young girl ant, an ant without a name, set off to climb the mountain and to push the boundaries of knowledge.

Before she set off, she was applauded by all the other ants, each one of whom had turned out to wish her luck.

The girl ant without a name told her mother and father that she loved them.

Then, showing no fear whatsoever, she marched over to the mountain and she began to climb.

Clustered in the shadow of the mountain, the other ants watched in awe. None of them had ever experienced a mountain before. Although the young ants were excited by it, the old ants were filled with dread.

The entire population watched as the tender young ant without a name climbed and climbed.

Up, up, up.

Zigzagging along the dark-green grooves, higher and higher into the heavens.

Clambering over a curve at the top, the ant without a name disappeared from view.

'She's been swallowed up by the mountain!' exclaimed a little boy at the front of the crowd.

'She's vanished into the sky!' chimed in another.

'No, no, no!' mused a kindly old ant at the back. 'She's still up there. We just can't see her because she's out of view.'

At the top of the melon, the tender ant without a name surveyed the geography of the mountain. Meticulous by nature, she sketched what she had found – a great turret of rock – which was of course the melon's stalk.

Then, once satisfied with her exploration of the mountain itself, the tender young girl ant without a name turned her back on the rock turret and gazed out into the distance.

Far down below, she spotted the entire ant population, all huddled together in a mass. From the great height they looked like tiny specks no bigger than, well, no bigger than ants.

At any other time during her short life, the tender young ant explorer would have marvelled at seeing every single ant she had ever known huddled there in one spot. But being at the top of the great mountain, marvelling at the other ants was the very last thing on her mind.

That was because over the vast, desolate plain, she had spied something more wonderful and more extraordinary than even the melon mountain at whose summit she was standing...

A sea of crystal water, its surface as sleek as burnished silver.

Standing there, her mouth wide open in awe, the tender girl ant without a name gazed and she gazed, as she wondered how the ant community could never have known that the inland sea was there at all.

As she surveyed the panorama, making careful notes as she did so, she came to realize the reason why the sea had never been discovered, even though it was close. Between where it lay, and the nest in which the ants lived, there was a deep ditch – known to one and all as 'the Precipice of Woe'.

Once her sketches and notes were complete, the tender ant without a name retraced her steps. And, with the great care of a meticulous character, she descended the cliff face to cheers and applause.

'How is it at the top of the great mountain?' cried an old ant.

'Is it as daunting up there as it looks?' hollered another.

'Weren't you frightened out of your wits?' cackled a third.

The tender girl ant without a name smiled politely at the throng, and held up a hand so as to silence them.

'I have something to tell you,' she said.

'Tell us!' all the ants cried out as one.

'Is it about the great mountain?!' cooed a little girl ant at the back.

'Of course it is!' called another. 'After all, the brave young ant explorer has just scaled it, as you saw!'

The tender young girl ant without a name smiled demurely and held up a hand a second time.

'I did indeed climb right up to the top,' she replied. 'And the great mountain is, well, it's a great mountain... but it's of no use to any of us.'

A murmur of disapproval rippled through the throng.

'We love the great mountain!' bawled an ant woman in the middle of the crowd. 'We love *our* great mountain!'

The tender young girl ant without a name held up a hand a third time.

'I am not suggesting for a moment that you do not love and adore the great mountain,' she responded. 'But what I have to tell you is that the use of the great mountain is not so much as a mountain itself, but as something else.'

The ant congregation seemed confused.

'If it's not a great mountain, then what is it?' spat an especially feisty ant.

'Yes!' wailed another. 'If it's not a great mountain, then what is it – what *is* the great mountain?!'

The tender young girl ant without a name smiled demurely a second time.

'It's a lookout point, from which I spied a natural wonder – a natural wonder that is to change all our lives.'

As the other ants listened, she explained that beyond the Precipice of Woe there lay a vast inland sea.

A communal gasp went up as the news was heard and digested.

And as it did, the tender young girl ant without a name held up her hand yet again.

'Before you ask me how we will ever breach the Precipice of Woe, I shall tell you. We build a bridge.'

'A bridge! A bridge!' the ants cried out. 'We'll build a bridge.'

A few days passed in which there was much activity.

First, all the ants worked together to make a bridge across the Precipice of Woe.

Next, an expeditionary force was dispatched to make sure the inland sea was not poisoned in some way. Once it was found to be fresh water, the ant population took it in turns to venture there to see it for themselves.

Then, when all the excitement was over, the tender young girl ant who had scaled the mountain and spied the inland sea was presented with a medal for services to exploration.

But best of all, she was given a name – Alice the Valiant.

In the fullness of time, ripened by adventure, Alice the Valiant became queen of the ants. And she ruled the vast plain, great mountain, and the inland sea, until she was called to ant heaven at the end of her days.

Melon Think

ONCE UPON A time, in the Land of Emerald Water, there lived a little girl called Clementine.

She was different from the other little girls in the valley.

Unlike the other girls, who liked pink, her favourite colour was red.

And unlike the other little girls, who wore plain dresses, her dress had daisies on the front.

And unlike the other little girls, whose favourite food was cheese, she liked watermelon.

Little Clementine absolutely adored watermelon.

Indeed, it was no exaggeration to say that watermelon was all she ever thought about, or wanted to eat.

From the moment she woke up in the morning until the moment she laid her head on the pillow at night, she babbled on and on about watermelons.

And when she wasn't babbling about them, she was gorging herself on them.

As Clementine grew older, her mother and father found themselves wondering why their beloved daughter was so attracted to the fruit. It was a question that was raised by her teachers in school, and one that her friends found themselves pondering as well.

Not wishing to offend Clementine, her parents, teachers, and friends would voice their concern with care.

Whenever any of them asked why the little girl had such an enthusiasm for watermelons, she would blush, then spout out a single, well-practised line:

'Melons make me very happy indeed.'

'But there are other fruits that taste as nice,' her mother would say.

'There are other things you could study in class,' her teachers would say.

'And there are other things you could talk about at break time,' her friends would say.

'I know that,' she would answer. 'But I want to eat watermelons and draw watermelons and talk about watermelons, because watermelons make me very happy indeed.'

Years passed.

Clementine grew from a little girl into a lovely young woman. It wasn't long before a stream of young men started appearing at the front door of her family home.

One by one, they asked whether Clementine would take a stroll with them through the forest, or go down to the water and skim stones at the riverbank.

And, one by one, Clementine politely refused.

'I'd rather stay here at home with this fine watermelon,' she would say. 'You see, it's as good a companion as I could ever wish to have.'

Concern having reached fever pitch, Clementine's parents sent for a physician. Invited into their home under the pretext that he was a distant relative passing through the Land of Emerald Water, the doctor made a careful observation of the young woman's condition.

After a full week of hearing Clementine babbling on about watermelons, of watching her sketching watermelons, and daydreaming about them too, he explained his diagnosis.

'Your dear daughter is suffering from what we call in psychological circles "Melon Think",' he said.

The mother looked at the father, and the father looked at the mother.

Both at once, they repeated the pair of words, a question mark at the end.

The physician dipped his head in a long, solemn nod.

'Is there a cure for the condition?' the father asked.

Again, the physician's head dipped.

'To recover, your dear daughter must do exactly as I say.'

The mother sighed.

'But if Clementine knows you're a medical man,' she said, 'she's sure to clam up. And, when she clams up, all she thinks about is watermelons.'

'A vicious melon circle,' the father muttered, his gaze focused on the middle distance.

'Fear not,' the physician answered, 'because I have a solution.'

Next day, when Clementine was sitting beside the fire sketching a plump, ripe watermelon, the family guest asked if she would help him.

'Help you with what?'

'With a matter that concerns a watermelon.'

Clementine's eyes sparkled as though she had heard wonders.

'It would be a pleasure,' she said.

Giving thanks, the visitor unfurled a pouch and tapped its contents onto the table set beside the fire.

Instantly, Clementine recognized the contents as a little mountain of dried melon seeds.

'They're so lovely,' she said.

'I took them from the most delicious melon I've ever eaten,' the visitor replied. 'And, with great care, I've dried them and made them ready.'

'Ready for planting?'

The guest shook his head.

'These seeds aren't for planting.'

'Then for eating?' probed Clementine.

'No, no,' said the visitor. 'Not for eating, either.'

'If they're not for planting or for eating, what could their purpose be?'

The guest grinned.

'They are part of a game,' he said. 'A game that I have invented, but which I want to test.'

In the hours that followed, Clementine was led through a mysterious keyhole into the magical world of the game the physician had invented right there and then.

A game he called 'Melon Think'.

The rules were not complex, but to win required extraordinary skill.

Her dainty green eyes reflecting the firelight, Clementine played and she played.

And she played and she played.

As she played, moving her dried melon seeds around the tabletop, she giggled and huffed, sighed, groaned, and slapped her hands together in delight.

All night she played, and all night the physician, who was posing as a visiting relative, watched.

For, as Clementine was sucked down through the levels of the game, she forgot about her love for watermelons.

When her father and mother came down for breakfast, they found their daughter engrossed in the very same game she had begun so many hours before.

The parents exchanged a glance with the physician.

He responded discreetly with a nod, and with half a wink.

Next day, Clementine stood at the door and bade farewell to the guest.

'What will you do with Melon Think?' she asked softly.

'The question is what *you* will do with it,' he replied.

'*Me?*'

'Indeed. *You*. I've left the pouch of dried melon seeds on the table, and am relying on you to tell everyone about it.'

Clementine blushed.

'That's such a responsibility,' she said.

'A responsibility of which you are quite worthy.'

'But who will I teach it to?'

'Anyone and everyone who's eaten their way through a watermelon, and who's been left with a little pile of seeds.'

With that, the physician put on his hat and strode away into the distance.

Although Clementine had got over her fixation with watermelons, she had embraced a new fixation – itself born of obsession.

In the days and weeks that followed, she taught Melon Think to her friends at school, and to the traders in the market, to the shepherds in the fields, and to the woodcutters in the deepest, darkest part of the forest.

Her friends taught the game to their friends, and the traders taught it to traders elsewhere. The shepherds in the fields taught it to all the other shepherds in the valley. And the woodcutters in the deepest, darkest part of the forest taught it to the carpenters who ventured there in search of wood.

Everyone who learned the game taught it to others.

They in turn passed it on... throughout the Land of Emerald Water, and far beyond.

Visit the markets, teahouses, palaces or ordinary homes, the riverbank or the forests, and you'll find the game being played by old and young.

The only person who no longer plays it is Clementine.

The thought of asking her why hasn't crossed a single mind.

Everyone else is too fixated on playing Melon Think to care.

A Melon Curse

ONCE UPON A time, there was a kingdom in which everyone was content.

The sun blazed down all day, and the stars twinkled all night.

The fields were filled with the finest melons.

In the villages and towns, the people were as happy as happy can be.

Even the witches were content.

Unlike witches elsewhere, they only cast good magic, seeking to make the populace even more content than they already were.

Each year, on the last day of the summer, all the people came together to give thanks for good fortune, and to feast on the melon crop. Seated at a low table in the capital, the king and queen presided over the festivities, the great and the good seated around them.

On the occasion about which we are concerned, the Red Witch – a favoured friend of the royal couple – took a choice piece of watermelon from the hand of the queen herself.

Giving thanks, the Red Witch devoured the succulent piece of fruit. And, when she had finished it, she praised the delicious taste.

On hearing the expression of pleasure, the king asked whether she would like another slice.

Turning to face her host, the Red Witch smiled.

'I would be absolutely delighted,' she said.

But rather than pass her another slice of melon as she had expected, the king did something that took everyone present by surprise.

He burst out laughing, then he laughed and he laughed…

…and he laughed and he laughed, his cheeks flushed redder than the reddest rose.

No one could understand why the monarch was quite so overcome. They looked at him in respectful silence – they didn't dare question the reason for such mirth.

Then, all of a sudden, a wizened old man pointed at the Red Witch. No sooner was his finger outstretched than he started laughing, too.

A moment after that, everyone present had dropped their melon slices, and was laughing like they had never laughed before.

The only person not howling with laughter was a little girl seated close by the Red Witch.

A little girl whose name was Amberine.

'It's your tooth!' she said tenderly. 'There's a watermelon seed caught in your teeth, so it looks as though you've lost your tooth!'

Unable to stand the embarrassment any longer, the Red Witch stood up and left. In all the laughter, and with so much fine watermelon to eat, no one noticed that she had gone.

No one, that is, except for Amberine, whose eyes had welled with tears at the way everyone was laughing at the kindly witch.

A few days passed.

Then a few more.

The last of the melons were brought in from the fields, and the people of the kingdom were more content than they had ever been.

Little did they know that their sense of contentment was about to change.

One morning, the king was washing in his dressing room when he caught a flash of himself in the mirror.

To his horror, his face was covered in grotesque warts, and a pair of horns had sprouted on either side of his head.

He was about to cry out in shock when he heard the sound of the queen screaming from her own dressing room.

Within a minute or two, an army of servants was scurrying to and fro, each of them howling in fear and in dread. For every soul in the palace had succumbed to the same grotesque condition of warts and devil horns.

As morning slipped into afternoon, the happy kingdom descended into despondency and gloom.

Without wasting a moment, the king called for his advisers to explain the condition.

'It's a disease sent by our enemies,' said the first.

'It's an affliction that's blown in over the ocean,' declared the second.

'It's an act of God,' intoned the third.

Scientists were sent to study random patients.

Spies were dispatched to neighbouring kingdoms.

Parsons were ordered to pray for a miraculous cure.

Every mirror in the kingdom was smashed, by order of the king.

Weeks passed, and nothing changed.

If anything, the warts grew worse, and some

people found that even more than two horns had sprouted from their heads in the night.

An air of utter misery overwhelmed the once happy kingdom.

The scientists and the spies had come up with nothing, and the parsons had prayed until they were hoarse.

The only person in the entire kingdom who was not covered head to toe in warts, and who hadn't sprouted horns, was little Amberine.

She lived in the forest with her grandmother, whose eyesight had failed with advanced age. On venturing to the market, she witnessed the affliction and the suffering. Not wishing her grandmother to think she was somehow different, Amberine pretended to be all covered in warts and to have sprouted horns along with everyone else.

While the scientists, the spies, and everyone else searched for answers, Amberine guessed what had taken place.

When her grandmother was taking an afternoon nap, she put on her coat, hurried through the forest, behind the waterfalls, up the crags, and down the steep sides of the next valley.

There, she eventually arrived at the trunk of an enormous tree, the rungs of a ladder nailed into it.

Without any trepidation, she ascended and, after much climbing, she reached a frail wooden dwelling cradled in its branches.

No sooner had Amberine arrived at the treehouse than she heard a voice.

'You've come to ask me to lift the melon curse, haven't you?'

'Dear Red Witch,' said the little girl politely, 'I can only imagine how much it hurt when they all laughed at you. But the spell you've cast is causing sorrow on a truly terrible scale.'

The Red Witch bristled, then shrugged.

'They should have thought before they ridiculed me,' she replied in a cold voice.

'But that's just it,' said Amberine, 'they *weren't* thinking. And that's why they were so offensive. People hurt the most when they don't think.'

The Red Witch widened her eyes.

'I have no sympathy for them,' she said.

On hearing the words, the little girl's eyes welled with tears once again.

'If you have no sympathy for them, at least have sympathy for *me*,' she said.

'But I do. It's the reason why I spared you. In case you haven't noticed, you don't have warts or horns.'

'That's just the point,' Amberine rejoined. 'And because you have spared me, I will become an outcast. With time I may even become an object of ridicule as well – because I am different from everyone else.'

The Red Witch combed a set of fingernails through her long grey hair.

'Then should I give you warts and horns, so that you blend in with all the rest?'

Puddles of tears welled in Amberine's eyes and tumbled down her cheeks.

'Punishing someone just to make them fit in seems crueller than cruel,' she said.

'No crueller than being mocked by everyone in the land!'

'By *almost* everyone,' the little girl corrected.

The Red Witch stared out at the forest, her mind reliving the public humiliation. She was about to say something when Amberine reached out and touched the witch's hand.

'The word in the capital is that our enemies are massing on the borders, planning to invade now that we're so sorrowful and weak.'

'*So?*'

'So… is it right that a kingdom be lost, all because someone with strength got a melon seed caught in her teeth?'

Again, the Red Witch stared out at the forest.

Her expression sullen, she let out a sigh.

'I suppose I've been foolish,' she said. 'But in my foolishness, I imagined I was clever as clever can be.'

'But you *are* clever,' Amberine replied.

'Why do you say that?'

'Because you know the only way to secure the future of the kingdom is to lift the spell.'

The Red Witch whispered a secret incantation to reverse the spell.

In the blink of an eye, every wart and every horn vanished.

Through days and nights, celebrations rang out.

Hearing the triumphant clamour of trumpets and drums, the enemies withdrew from the borders.

Contentment and peace returned to the kingdom.

Never again did the Red Witch use a spell in anger.

As for Amberine, she grew into a fine young woman who, with the fullness of time, set out on the most extraordinary adventure.

But that's another story.

The Melon That Would Be King

ONCE UPON A time, when the moon was still in love with the sun, there was a kingdom beyond the horizon called the Land of Forbidden Hope.

In all the city streets, the mountains, forests, fields, and farmsteads, the melon-people who resided there were pleased with their lot.

No matter whether rich or poor, every single melon knew their fortune – a fortune derived from the fact that the king was a good one, and that the queen was twice as kind.

One morning in the height of summer, trumpets resounded on the battlements of the great castle in which the royal melon family dwelt.

Every melon hurried to the central square so as to hear the proclamation that was about to be made.

Striding out from the castle's keep, an equerry to the king unfurled a scroll and read in his loudest voice:

'Let it be known that at dawn this morning, Her Majesty the Queen of the Land of Forbidden Hope gave birth to a son. The radiant baby, who shall be known as Prince Cantaloupe, shall be heir to the throne.'

Cheers rang out through the streets, and the melon people rejoiced as they had never rejoiced before.

In the coming weeks, months, and years, Prince Cantaloupe grew from a babe in arms to a fine little boy, as kind and courteous as he was lovely to the eye.

Now, it just so happened that the chief vizier had a son who bore a startling physical resemblance to Prince Cantaloupe. Indeed, it was said by one and all that the two were identical – which of course they were not. While in appearance they were very similar, one was of royal birth, and the other most definitely was not.

The vizier's son, whose name was Galia, may have resembled Prince Cantaloupe in every way, but he was not kind or courteous at all. Indeed, Galia was monstrous – causing problems for everyone and anyone who ever encountered him.

When both Prince Cantaloupe and Galia were about four melon years old, the vizier had an idea. If he were to swap his son for the prince, in the fullness of time his offspring would become king.

And so, acting on his plan, the vizier did indeed exchange his son for the crown prince, having explained to the little melon boy exactly what he was doing. Then, once Prince Cantaloupe had been exchanged, the wicked vizier sent the royal child to live with a hunter in the depths of the forest.

As wily by nature as his father, little Galia pretended to be the crown prince. He was so good at feigning, the royal household didn't suspect for a moment that he was an imposter. Whenever anyone enquired as to the whereabouts of his son, the vizier simply answered that he had gone to the countryside to stay with a distant aunt.

At first, Prince Cantaloupe had persuaded the old man that he was none other than the heir to the throne. But, since it seemed so implausible to the hunter's ears, and since they were so far from anyone else, he got on with life with the hunter.

Time passed.

As it did so, Prince Cantaloupe learned how to hunt and fish.

Over months and years, the hunter taught him stories that contained a wealth of knowledge, and passed on all manner of secrets his own father had passed to him.

With time, Prince Cantaloupe blossomed as a young man, and was eager to go in search of adventure. He had now lived with the hunter for so long that he no longer missed his parents, or the grandeur of court life. Rather, he had become used to a far simpler existence.

Thanking the hunter for his kindness and all the life lessons, Prince Cantaloupe set off one bright morning, a knapsack slung over his rounded shoulder.

He hadn't travelled far from the forest when he came to a shack in which a weaver lived with his wife.

'Who are you and where are you going?' asked the weaver.

'I am a humble hunter's son,' said Cantaloupe, 'and I am going in search of adventure.'

Remembering a time when he was young, the weaver fumbled in his pocket and pulled out a spindle.

'This looks like an ordinary spindle,' he said, 'but in actual fact it's magical. In a time of need, kiss your lips to the spindle, and the cotton will become the strongest twine in existence.'

Expressing most sincere thanks, Prince Cantaloupe spent the night at the weaver's shack, then continued next morning on his journey.

Next day, he crossed the horizon, and another, and eventually arrived at a mountain.

There, in a cleft among the rocks, he found a hermit.

'Who are you and where are you going?' asked the hermit.

'I am Cantaloupe, the son of a humble hunter,' he said, 'and I am going in search of adventure.'

Remembering a time when he was young, the hermit fumbled in his pocket and pulled out a chicken bone.

'This looks like an ordinary chicken bone,' he said, 'but in actual fact it's magical. In a time of need, touch it to your chin, and a legion of tigers will appear. They will help you in any way they can.'

Expressing most sincere thanks, Prince Cantaloupe left the hermit and continued on his journey.

He climbed the mountain and crossed a desert.

Then, one morning, he reached a river on whose bank a fisherman was sitting with his rod.

'Who are you and where are you going?' asked the fisherman.

'I am a humble hunter's son,' said Cantaloupe, 'and I am going in search of adventure.'

Remembering a time when he was young, the fisherman fumbled in his pocket and pulled out a little tin.

'This looks like an ordinary tin,' he said, 'but in actual fact it's magical. In a time of need, open the tin. You will find a pod in which there are two beans. Whoever swallows one of the beans will be transported to the ends of the earth.'

Expressing his most sincere thanks, Prince Cantaloupe left the fisherman and continued on his journey.

A little farther, beyond forests and fields, the traveller encountered a farmer.

'Who are you and where are you going?' asked the farmer.

'I am Cantaloupe, a humble hunter's son,' he said, 'and I am going in search of adventure.'

Remembering a time when he was young, the farmer fumbled in his pocket and pulled out a nail.

'This looks like an ordinary nail,' he said, 'but in actual fact it's magical. Hold it in your fist when in need, and you will turn invisible. To be seen once again, blow on it, and the magic will dissipate.'

Expressing most sincere thanks, Prince Cantaloupe continued on his journey.

After many adventures, he reached a land in which all the melons were fearful of their leader.

Taking lodgings in a caravanserai, he learned that the king was a despot, and that he planned to invade a kingdom far to the west.

A blacksmith at the caravanserai who was passing on the information shook his head in sorrow.

'Those poor melons in the Land of Forbidden Hope,' he said.

Prince Cantaloupe frowned.

'What about them?'

The blacksmith shrugged.

'Well, our poor melon brothers and sisters there are going to be invaded.'

A shock of horror surged through Prince Cantaloupe's spine. All he could think of was that he had to warn his father, the king.

But there was no time.

For the despotic leader of the land to which he had travelled was about to dispatch his army – an army that rode fleet-footed horses as swift as the wind.

Prince Cantaloupe was wondering what to do when the blacksmith mumbled something which gave him an idea.

'The king is searching for last-minute recruits for his army.'

No sooner had the sentence been spoken, than Prince Cantaloupe set off for the barracks at which the invading army was massing.

Having been raised by the huntsman, he was able to prove his expertise with a gun. Within the hours of a single day, he was in uniform and had been assigned to the advance reconnaissance unit.

Once the fighting force was ready, the brave young melons of the advance team were dispatched. Mounting his steed, Prince Cantaloupe found it was indeed fleet-footed.

Through days and nights the creature galloped, not resting for a single moment – not until it reached the edge of a forest, the very same one in which the hunter lived.

At a makeshift camp, the general of the invading army harangued his men. Warning them to embrace the war that was to follow, he asked for a volunteer – a volunteer to survey the capital so that an invasion plan could be devised.

No sooner had the call been given than Prince Cantaloupe stepped forward.

'I shall do it!' he exclaimed.

The general made note of the bravery.

'You are the best shot,' he said. 'Let good fortune be with you.'

Under the cover of darkness, Prince Cantaloupe set off.

By the first strains of morning light, he had reached the Land of Forbidden Hope. Although separated from his birthplace for so long, he was deeply moved at having returned.

Prince Cantaloupe surveyed the outskirts of the capital and discovered a cliff running to the south. Thinking fast, he took the spindle the weaver had given him from his pocket. Pressing it to his lips, it turned into a reel of twine.

Then, paying the twine out at ankle level, he ran it from tree to tree at the end of the cliff.

Next, he hurried back to the encampment and gave his report.

'We must come in from the south,' he said, 'the fortifications are weakest there. But there are lookouts, and so we would do best to attack under the cover of darkness.'

Congratulating the brave young melon, the general drew up the invasion plans.

In the dead of night, the vast fighting force set off.

A crescent moon as witness, the melon army pushed forwards.

When they were half a mile from the cliff, Prince Cantaloupe rode back, as if checking the rear lines. Once behind all the other troops, he took the chicken bone from his pocket. Touching it to his chin, he conjured the legion of tigers that the hermit had promised would come.

'Drive the soldiers towards the cliff!' he cried.

As soon as the order was given, the tigers surged ahead.

In a crazed hullabaloo of teeth and claws, they chased every last soldier to the cliff. Enveloped in darkness and scared out of their wits, the soldiers sprinted hither and thither, before tripping over the twine and careening over the precipice.

With the army dispatched, Prince Cantaloupe took the nail from his pocket and blew on it, as the farmer had instructed him to do.

Instantly, he was rendered invisible.

Once so, he made his way through the capital and up to the palace.

First, he crept into the apartment in which the vizier was fast asleep.

Opening the tin the fisherman had given him, he squeezed one of the beans from the pod, and forced it down the vizier's throat.

No sooner had it been ingested than the wretched vizier vanished, transported to the ends of the earth.

Then, still rendered invisible, Prince Cantaloupe crept into the royal apartment and into his own bedroom. Tucked up under the blankets in his own bedstead was the imposter.

Taking the second bean from the tin, he pressed it down the throat of the vizier's son.

As with his father, the youth vanished – transported to the ends of the earth.

Lastly, Prince Cantaloupe took out the nail which the farmer had given him.

Blowing on it, he was rendered visible. Having washed himself, he went to the cupboard, took out a set of pyjamas, and climbed into bed.

Despite saving the kingdom, never once did Prince Cantaloupe reveal how he had been swapped as a child, or raised by a hunter in the forest.

...Or how, by twists and turns, he had saved the Land of Forbidden Hope.

The Square Melon

FOR A THOUSAND years, melons had been grown at the base of the Sleek Mountains.

For a thousand years of perfect soil.

For a thousand years of glorious irrigation.

For a thousand years of shelter from the wind.

For a thousand years of peace.

In all that time, millions of plump, round melons with golden-yellow skin grew in the mountains' shade.

Some melons were smaller or larger than the others.

Some were lighter or darker than the rest.

But never was there a melon as strange as the one that appeared at the base of the Sleek Mountains at such-and-such a time – a melon that is the hero of this story.

It all began when an ordinary farmer was rooting

through a storeroom containing outdated farming supplies. His wife had nagged him to clear out the building so it could be used for something else.

While tossing out a mass of old crates and ploughs, flowerpots and seed trays, he noticed something in the corner of the storeroom.

A wooden box, the sides of which were adorned with a curious geometric design.

Curious as to what might be inside, the farmer took it out into the light, blew off the dust, and opened the lid.

Inside, packed in a strand of cloth, was a melon seed.

Beneath it was a scrap of paper. Squinting, the farmer managed to make out three lines of scribbled text:

Plant me with the melon crop
And watch as a new order is revealed
Because tranquillity breeds weakness.

171

Shrugging, the farmer wondered what kind of practical joke it could be.

He was about to flick the seed into the gutter when he remembered something from his childhood...

While seated on his grandfather's knee one morning, he'd heard a tale of how a single melon seed had changed the world.

Curious as to what effect such a tiny thing might have, the farmer did as the message demanded, and planted the seed in the middle of his field.

Weeks passed, and he quite forgot about the box, the message, and the seed.

Then, one day, while out surveying the melon crop, he set eyes on it...

A melon with a ripe golden skin and a fine green stalk – but a melon quite unlike any other he had ever seen.

You see, the melon in question was square.

Bewildered, the farmer just stood there in astonishment, mouth wide open and hand on head.

Having gaped in front of the melon for a good long while, he wondered what to do. For a moment he thought of clipping it off the vine and taking it home.

But, as he turned it around in his head, he realized there would be a thousand questions from the other melon farmers in the valley.

Like everyone else for a hundred miles, they were mad about melons. The farmer knew full well that each and every one of them would want to know how such a thing as a square melon could ever have appeared at the base of the Sleek Mountains.

While the farmer stood there, umming and ahhing at what to do, a soldier from the king's guard galloped past the field. Hoping to be invited for refreshments, the soldier stopped, dismounted, and made his way to where the farmer was standing.

As the soldier strode through the rows of melons, the farmer pulled off his turban and threw it over the square melon.

Suspicious by nature, the soldier gave greetings, and enquired what the turban was covering.

'Nothing,' answered the farmer.

Frowning, the soldier tugged the cloth away, and his mouth gaped open wide.

'What devilry is this?!' he cried.

'I have no idea why it is like that,' the farmer said.

'I have cause to believe you have been involved in black magic!' he snapped.

And with that, the soldier from the king's guard bound the farmer's hands behind his back, clipped the melon from its vine, and took them both to the palace.

The farmer was dragged to the dungeon; the melon was borne to the throne room, where the king was informed directly of what had transpired.

Sitting on his throne, he asked for the man who had grown a square melon to be brought.

Fawning and wailing with sorrow, the farmer was

dragged from the dungeon and kicked to the floor a few feet away from the king.

'Explain yourself!' hissed the vizier.

'Your Majesty!' exclaimed the farmer. 'I've farmed that field at the base of the Sleek Mountains as my father did, and his father before him. I am a humble God-fearing man with no education. All I have ever known is growing melons… growing *round* melons. Never once have I seen, or even imagined, such a thing as this!'

The king wasn't listening.

Beckoning his vizier to approach, he whispered in his ear:

'As you know, we have enemies,' he said. 'Enemies who are quite devious enough to create a square melon… a square melon in which they could insert a bomb!'

A moment later, the farmer was dragged back to the dungeon, and the melon was taken there as well, and given a cell of its own.

Again, the king beckoned the adviser to come close.

His lips an inch from the obsequious vizier's ear, he said:

'Get a special unit of suicidal soldiers assembled, and have them examine the square melon. If they are blown to smithereens, reward them posthumously with medals.'

'And what if they are *not* blown to smithereens, Majesty?'

The king balked at the thought.

'Then have a special unit of scientists assembled, so that they can determine why the melon is square.'

Accordingly, a special unit of suicide soldiers was taken to the cell in which the melon was kept.

The door was unlocked.

Pushed inside, they were ordered to make a thorough examination of the melon.

By nature suicidal rather than brave, they took it

in turns to tap it and to yell at it, to poke it, and even to thump it with their fists.

Dejected at not having been blown to smithereens, they called out through the inspection hatch.

Within the hour, the suicide squad were back in their barracks, and the special unit of scientists were being led to the dungeons.

Armed with all manner of ingenious devices, they were given a few minutes each to drill down into the melon to make a full examination of the outer surface, flesh, and seeds.

One at a time, they announced their findings – that the melon was unremarkable except for the fact that it was square, and for the fact that it tasted sweeter and more succulent than any melon any of the scientists had ever grown.

The information was relayed to the throne room, and was passed from the vizier's lips to the royal ear.

'Have the melon brought up from the dungeon!' the king commanded.

The order was transmitted at speed.

In less time than it takes to tell, having been polished with a cloth and placed upon a velvet cushion, the melon was borne ceremoniously into the throne room once again.

Carried up to the throne upon which the monarch was seated, the fruit was inspected.

'Who ever thought of such a thing as a square melon?!' the king chuckled.

The vizier glided up.

'Would His Imperial Majesty wish to sample a slice?'

The king thought for a moment.

'Very well, cut a piece,' he said.

A golden knife was brought in by the king's personal melon chef. Expertly, he prepared a perfect slice.

Well aware of palace protocol, he passed it to the taster-in-chief.

The taster tasted, and gave a nod.

Only then was the slice of square melon ushered to the king.

A cube of the fruit, no larger than a die, was cut from the end and skewered by a fork.

In their own time, the king's lips parted.

The melon entered the royal mouth, the fork withdrew, and the lips closed.

A short interval came and went.

As though a spell had been cast, the king leapt up from his throne.

'My goodness!' he called out. 'I don't believe it! What an absolutely astonishing taste!'

Having expected condemnation, the vizier did a double-take.

Before he could utter a word, the imperial ruler ordered for the farmer to be freed from the dungeon and rewarded with a mountain of gold.

When this had been done, the king ordered for the seeds of the square melon to be gathered, and planted in the palace grounds.

Day and night, the king sat at the window of his apartment, a telescope in hand, watching as the crop of melons grew...

...and grew.

Although there was no certainty as to what would occur, every single fruit in the crop was square as well.

Within a matter of weeks, the fruits were harvested. Elated at the triumph of oddity, and the explosion of taste, the king ordered for the melons to be distributed to both rich and poor.

In every corner of the kingdom, seeds from the new square melons were planted.

And, beneath rain and sun, they grew.

Very soon, every single melon in the land was square.

Rejoicing, the people praised the king.

As for the farmer, he was lauded for having grown the original square melon.

Time passed.

Being as people are, everyone grew used to the sight of square melons, and to the sweet taste.

In the teahouses, old-timers would gather during the long, hot afternoons and reminisce.

'What a shame we no longer have the lovely old round melons of our youth,' they would say. 'They may not have been so pretty to look at, or quite so sweet, but they were what we knew and what we loved.'

The nostalgia swelled a little more each week.

And, eventually, the vizier caught wind of it.

Fearful that the monarchy itself might be affected by the unrest from melon nostalgia, the adviser sought an urgent audience with the king.

'Your Majesty,' he cooed, his tone unusually sycophantic, 'it appears as though the people are tiring of the new convention.'

'What new convention?!' the monarch barked, as a cube of succulent square melon was fed to him.

The vizier cocked his head at the end of the fork.

'*That*, Your Majesty,' he said.

The monarch erupted into an explosion of rage.

'In an act of largesse as great as any, I have given my damned people the most delicious and most practical foodstuff in the history of fruit!'

The vizier squirmed.

'It seems as though they're missing the old melons, Your Majesty, the old round melons that they had always known.'

Again, the king erupted.

'Let it be known that anyone who's heard complaining about the square melons will be publicly flogged!' he howled.

Days passed, in which the royal decree was nailed up in every market and teahouse. Fearful at the prospect of being flogged, the citizens bit their tongues.

But in secret each one of them missed the round melons.

One, an old woman, marched to the palace gates, a square melon in her wizened old hands.

As the guards looked on, she held the melon above her head, and thrust it as hard as she could onto the ground.

'That's what I think of the wretched new square melons!' she exclaimed.

The next thing she knew, she was being clapped in chains by guards and was dragged into the main square to be publicly flogged.

No one dared speak out.

Not at first, at any rate.

As the guard's whip was raised for the first of fifty lashes, someone hurled a square melon out of the window of their home.

Another square melon followed it.

And another.

Soon, the streets were covered in smashed square melons.

Spirits boosted by insurrection, the people ran from their houses and stormed the palace, flinging chunks of square melon at the guards.

By the end of the day, the king had been ousted, and had fled.

The people went back to the round melons which they knew and loved.

Every last square melon seed was gathered up and burnt.

This all happened a long, long time ago.

Venture to the kingdom at the base of the Sleek Mountains, and you won't see a square melon, because there aren't any to be found.

But listen, and you'll hear people telling stories about them in the teahouses.

…Stories about the time melons were square.

As for the farmer, he went back to his ordinary life, and everyone forgot the part he had played in the melon fiasco.

During the purge of square melons, he had kept a single seed.

Wrapping it in a strand of cloth, he scribbled a message, and placed it in the very same box he had found all those months before.

When his nagging wife wasn't looking, he scraped away a little dirt from the corner of the storeroom and buried the box.

It's still there now, awaiting a time when the order of life needs to be shaken up so that it may begin a new adventure.

Finis

A REQUEST

If you enjoyed this book, please review it on your favourite online retailer or review website.

Reviews are an author's best friend.

To stay in touch with Tahir Shah, and to hear about his upcoming releases before anyone else, please sign up for his mailing list:

✉ http://tahirshah.com/newsletter

And to follow him on social media, please go to any of the following links:

🐦 http://www.twitter.com/humanstew

📷 @tahirshah999

f http://www.facebook.com/TahirShahAuthor

▶ http://www.youtube.com/user/tahirshah999

𝓟 http://www.pinterest.com/tahirshah

g https://www.goodreads.com/tahirshahauthor

http://www.tahirshah.com